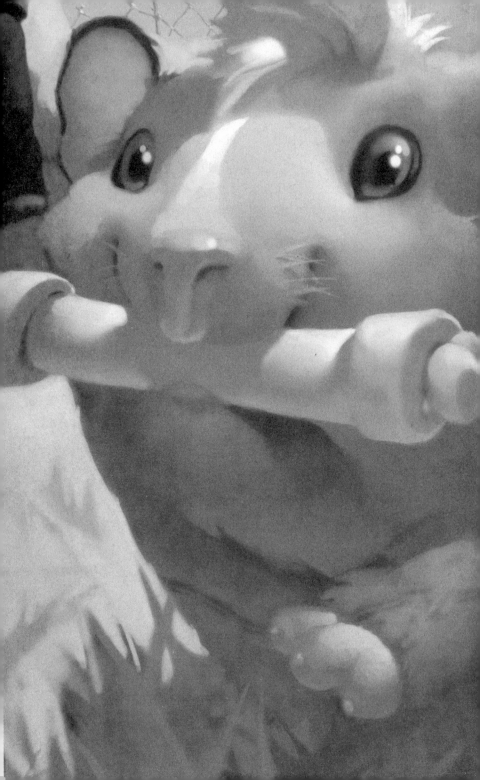

GUINEA
DOG

Patrick Jennings

EGMONT
USA
NEW YORK

EGMONT

We bring stories to life

First published by Egmont USA, 2010
443 Park Avenue South, Suite 806
New York, NY 10016

This novel is based on the short story "The Guinea Dog," by Patrick Jennings,
which originally appeared in the magazine *Storyworks*, January 2005.

3 5 7 9 8 6 4

www.egmontusa.com
www.patrickjennings.com

Library of Congress Cataloging-in-Publication Data
Jennings, Patrick.
Guinea dog / Patrick Jennings
p. cm.
Summary: When his mother brings home a guinea pig instead of the dog he has always wanted,
fifth-grader Rufus is not happy—until the rodent starts acting exactly like a dog.
ISBN 978-1-60684-053-5 (hardcover)—ISBN 978-1-60684-069-6 (reinforced library binding ed.)
[1. Guinea pigs—Fiction. 2. Family life—Fiction. 3. Schools—Fiction.] I. Title.
PZ7.J4298715Gu 2010
[Fic]—dc22
2009025117

Book design by Becky Terhune

Printed in the United States of America

CPSIA tracking label information:
Random House Production · 1745 Broadway · New York, NY 10019

For Soobie and Barry

Contents

1. I wanted a dog.

I didn't see anything wrong with that. People all over the world had dogs. My best friend had one. So did my worst friend. A lot of people had more than one. Our next-door neighbors had two. The family down the street had three.

People like dogs. Why? Because dogs rock. They learn tricks. They play games, like Fetch and Tug-of-War and Frisbee. They hang out with you. They run alongside your bike. They sleep at the foot of your bed. They protect you and your family from intruders. Some dogs even save people's lives. Who *wouldn't* want one?

Dad.

"Dogs are filthy and smelly, Rufus," Dad said yesterday when I asked him for the jillionth time why I couldn't have a dog. "Are you capable of keeping a dog free of grime and stench? Do you have that skill set? You can't even remember to put your dirty clothes in the hamper. I have to do it." Then he shuddered.

Smelliness is only one of Dad's reasons why I can't ever have a dog. His list is endless:

- They whine.
- They gnaw.
- They scratch.
- They bark.
- They beg.
- They jump up.
- They dig.
- They shed.
- They slobber.
- They drool.
- They lick people's faces.
- They lick themselves.
- They lick other dogs.
- They piddle everywhere, and that includes indoors.
- They poop everywhere, including indoors.

- Their poop has to be scooped.
- They eat shoes.
- They eat mice.
- They eat computer mice.
- They eat dead things.
- They eat poop.
- Their breath smells like dead things and poop.
- They have to be walked.
- They have to be walked in the middle of the night.
- They have to be walked in rain and snow and hail and sleet.
- They stop every two seconds to sniff.
- They tug on the leash.
- They chase cats, squirrels, birds, deer, and other dogs.
- They tramp mud into the house.
- They drag dead animals into the house.
- They infest the house with blood-sucking fleas.
- They get worms.
- They get rabies.
- They need shots. (And shots aren't free.)

- They chase cars.
- They get run over by cars. (Vet bills are expensive.)
- They eat tons of (expensive) dog food.
- They must be boarded in (expensive) kennels when their owners go away.
- They knock over Christmas trees.
- They attack mail carriers.
- They attack their owners.
- They attack their own tails.
- They are needy.
- They are clingy.
- They are high maintenance.
- They love people who don't love them.
- Etc.

Let's face it, I will never get a dog, not as long as I live with Dad in this clean, quiet, boring, stupid house. But just wait till I grow up. Then I will have the greatest, *awesomest* dog that ever lived and Dad won't be able to do anything about it. Take that, Dad!

But I don't want to wait till I'm grown up. I want a dog *now*.

Mom was never any help. So I didn't see how it could hurt to bug her about it again when she got home from work. Her job was mixing paint at Try Your Best Hardware. She'd been doing it for years and years.

"Your dad is the one who would be with the dog all day," she answered. "It's his call, I'm afraid."

My dad started working at home a few months before. He had taken a new job as an editor for a golf e-zine. That meant that not only was he home, like, 24/7, but also that he did most of the housework. Which was why he nagged me about my dirty clothes.

He had always been a pretty naggy, fussy guy, with all his lists of why he didn't like this or that, but being at home all the time had transformed him into Super Insane Fussy Work-at-Home Dad Guy.

"I'm sorry, sunshine," Mom said, patting me on the shoulder.

Then suddenly she brightened up.

"Hey! How about a *guinea pig*?"

This was classic Mom. "Lateral thinking,"

she called it. "Thinking outside of the box." If a door is slammed in your face, don't stand there banging on it. Don't beg someone to open it, or sulk or whine, or say the world isn't fair. Don't be a Zax. (It's a character in her favorite Dr. Seuss story.) Step aside and find another way in—a different door, or maybe a window.

"Guinea pigs don't bark," she explained. "They don't get fleas, or chew things up. They don't have to be walked. And they bathe themselves!"

"But Mom, I don't want a guinea pig. A guinea pig can't learn tricks, or run alongside your bike, or play Tug-of-War, or scare away intruders. I want a *dog*."

She kept on smiling. I don't think she heard me. We should have her hearing tested.

I'm sure she meant well. Her problem was just that she thought *too* laterally, *too* outside the box. Sometimes a person only wanted *one* particular thing and that was it. There was no point in suggesting anything else. For example:

I wanted a dog, a whole dog, and nothing but a dog.

On the way home from work the next day, Mom stopped at a pet store and bought a guinea pig.

2. It was orangish-brown, pudgy, and had a spiky white mohawk.

Its pink nose twitched like a rabbit's.

"Well, here she is, Rufus," Mom said. "Your new pet!"

"She?" I said. I don't know why, but I'd always imagined my dog would be a he.

"Yes, she's a sow," she said, smiling ear to ear.

People use that expression a lot, but my mom really does smile from one ear to the other. The corners of her mouth were, like, a nanometer from her ears.

Dad walked in. He was wearing his usual gray suit with a white shirt and tie. Just because he worked at home, he always said, didn't mean he couldn't look professional. I wondered if looking professional meant wearing fuzzy blue slippers.

"What's this?" he asked, his eyes locking on the rodent Mom had brought home.

"It's Rufus's new guinea pig!" she announced.

"*New* guinea pig?" Dad said. "I don't recall Rufus ever having an *old* guinea pig."

Dad's a stickler for speaking "precisely." Must be all the editing.

"My bad," Mom said. "I meant that I bought Rufus *a* guinea pig. For a pet. Instead of a dog."

Dad gave her the Stony Stare. The Stony Stare, which he uses a lot, means, *I don't need to say what I'm upset about*.

"I know I didn't discuss it with you," Mom said, her smile shrinking the tiniest bit, "but Rufus has been so miserable about not being allowed to have a dog, and a guinea pig seemed the perfect solution."

The Stony Stare continued.

"Guinea pigs don't bark," Mom explained

again. "They don't whine or drool or beg or get fleas or chew things up. And they don't have to be walked!"

Her smile stretched bigger than ever. The corners reached past her ears and into her hair. Honest.

Dad slowly shifted his eyes to the pig. It was in a metal cage with a green plastic tray on the bottom, and there was a little green plastic ramp inside that led up to a little green plastic loft. There was also a food dish with wilted lettuce in it and a water bottle attached to the bars, upside down.

"It does poop, I assume," Dad said.

"Of course she poops!" Mom laughed. "Everyone poops!"

"And who scoops the poop?" Dad asked, looking at me.

"Mom brought it home, not me," I said.

"Oh, they're just teeny little poops," Mom said. "Teeny pellets, like a rabbit's. They don't even smell. And she piddles in the bedding—which is made of recycled paper, by the way, Art."

She was kissing up. Dad's way into recycling. When he sweeps, he picks out little pieces of paper and plastic and puts them in the appropriate bins. He sorts through the garbage, too, and, boy, does he get sore if he finds anything recyclable in there, like a tag off a new shirt, or the little plastic thing it was attached with. Personally, I think he's into it so much because it makes him feel like he's doing something more important than just cleaning house. I don't think he's happy being a homemaker.

Mom turned to me and said, "They said at the pet store you should clean the cage whenever it starts to stink, which will be about once a week. Plus, you'll have to do some spot cleaning, when necessary."

I gave her the Stony Stare.

"Oh, and Art," she said, "guinea pigs are so *clean*. They bathe *themselves*. With their *tongues*."

"Too much information, Raquel," Dad said with a wince.

"Guinea pigs are strict vegetarians, so Dad

will collect scraps while he's preparing meals," Mom said. "Just like for a real pig."

"Oh, I will, will I?" Dad said.

"You'll have to feed and water her, too, of course, Rufus," Mom said. "Every day."

Having a guinea pig sounded about as much fun as having a pet fern.

"Did you hear that, Rufus?" Dad said. "The guinea pig is your responsibility. Are you up to it?"

I shrugged. "I don't know."

"Of course he is!" Mom said. "So it's okay, Art? We can keep her?"

Dad sighed loudly. "If Rufus keeps the cage clean and doesn't let the little monster out . . . and if I don't ever have to see it or hear it or know it exists—"

He sneered at the guinea pig as if it were a poop pellet.

"—then . . . well . . . okay, he can keep it. In his room." He looked at me. "But then no more begging for a dog, right?"

"But—" I began.

"YAY!" Mom squealed.

My dream of a dog died then and there. Instead, I was the proud owner/caretaker of a plump, punk guinea sow. Yippee.

How did Mom get away with stuff like this?

"So what are you going to name her, Rufus?" Mom asked. "I've been calling her Emmeline, but she's yours. You get to name her."

Mom was now not only smiling as wide as a hippopotamus, but her eyes were actually watering. Obviously the woman didn't get enough excitement in her life.

"Fido," I said. "That's what I was going to call my dog."

Mom laughed so suddenly and loud I almost swallowed my tongue.

"Oh, Rufus! You are *too* funny! 'Fido' is perfect! I love it!"

And she bent down and hugged me. Hard. I tolerated it. At last she let me go.

"Well?" she asked. "What do you say?"

Though I was not grateful to her in the slightest—in fact, I was pretty mad at her—I said, "Thanks, Mom."

She hugged me again, even harder than

the first time. I feared for my life.

When she released me, I saw she was crying. For real.

Over a guinea pig.

"You're welcome, sunshine," she said to me, her chin quivering. "I knew you'd love her!"

I picked up Fido's cage, carried it up to my room, kicked some of my junk aside, then dropped the cage on the floor. My fern made herself at home. She waddled around her cage. She piddled. She pooped. Then she piddled again. Then, just for fun, she pooped again.

So much for clean "Emmeline."

3. I was dreaming I had a rottweiler.

It was the best dream I ever had. Then the guinea pig woke me up right in the middle of it.

She was gripping the bars of her cage with her tiny pink paws and screeching like bad bike brakes.

I heard a knock on the door. I was pretty sure who it was.

"Come in, Dad."

The door swung open. Dad was wearing his fuzzy blue slippers and his plaid robe over his yellow pinstriped pajamas. His hair was messed up. His eyes were puffy. He was grimacing. He didn't come in. He refuses to set foot in the Dump, which is what he calls my room.

"What is that awful sound?" he asked.

I pointed at Fido. "Why, it's the quiet, clean pet Mom bought me."

"It's unacceptable," he said.

I nodded.

Mom appeared behind him, pouting. "I think Emmeline's lonely."

"Fido," I reminded her.

"Why don't you take her out of her cage and let her sleep in bed with you, Rufus?"

I looked at Dad and we had a rare moment of seeing eye to eye: my mom—his wife—was a loon.

"Well, then, I'll do it," she said.

She bent down and opened the door of the cage. Fido stopped whining and scurried out. She raced over to my bed and started tugging on the blanket.

"There, see?" Mom said smugly.

She scooped Fido up and set her on the bed. The rodent's little tongue spilled out of her mouth. She wagged her nonexistent tail. She ran up my body and licked my chin.

"Oh, she *loves* you," Mom said, beaming.

I tried to smile back, but I couldn't make it work.

"If she'll be quiet, fine, she can be out of her cage," Dad said.

"She'll be quiet," Mom said.

Fido then dashed to the foot of my bed and curled up at my feet.

"Just as snug as a bug in a rug!" Mom said.

"Ugh," said Dad, and left.

I was with him on that. Mom has a way of talking sometimes that makes you want to throw up.

"Night-night, Rufus," Mom whispered, and tiptoed out.

Like that. It's like living trapped inside Missus Rogers' Neighborhood.

She can't seem to grasp that I'm not three years old anymore. I wonder if she ever will.

Now that I was alone—well, almost—I closed my eyes and went back to sleep. I was hoping the rottweiler dream would reboot, but instead I dreamed I was running in one of those hamster exercise wheels.

🐾 🐾 🐾

Fido was still there at my feet when I woke up in the morning. The second she realized I was awake, though, she ran at my face and slobbered it all up.

That was weird to wake up to.

"Cut it out!" I whined. "Down!"

She cut it out. And sat down. Her tongue fell out of her mouth and she sat there gaping up at me like she was waiting for my next command. Which was also weird.

I slipped out from under the covers and flipped them over on her. She scrambled frantically underneath them, trying to get out. Then she gave up and started screeching really loud.

"Quiet!" I said.

This command she ignored.

I got dressed with my fingers in my ears— not an easy thing to do. There was a knock on the door.

"Come in, Dad."

Dad pushed the door open. He gave me the Stony Stare. He kept his toes outside the Dump's border.

"It's not my fault," I said.

He kept staring.

"Oh, all right," I said.

I uncovered Fido. She stopped screeching and started wagging her hairy butt.

"Don't do that again," Dad said.

"Copy that," I said.

"Breakfast is ready."

"Copy that, too."

"Copy that" was my new favorite way of saying "okay," replacing "Gotcha, chief," which Dad recently made me stop saying.

"Put the rat back in its cage. I do not want it in my kitchen."

"Copy that."

I lifted Fido up—she was lighter than I thought she'd be, considering how fat she looked—put her in her cage, and locked the door. She grabbed the bars and screeched.

Dad covered his ears and yelled, "Take her back out! Take her back out! Take her out! Out, out!"

Dad is one major freaker outer.

"Copy that," I said, and took her out of

her cage. She stopped screeching.

Dad breathed a mighty sigh.

"I'll bring your breakfast up to you."

This was a bit of a shock. I was under strict orders never to bring food into my room. But I answered, "Copy that."

"Stop saying 'Copy that,'" Dad said.

"I can't say 'Copy that,' either?"

"No."

He never lets me have any fun. "Okay," I said. "I'll say 'Okay.'"

Dad sighed again, then sneered at Fido, and left. He returned a few minutes later carrying a tray with a plate of scrambled eggs, sausage, and buttered toast on it, plus a glass of OJ. Fido began to pant and whimper.

"Do not give that animal any food," Dad said firmly.

"Copy—" I started to say, then caught myself. "Okay."

Dad left and I sat on my bed and started wolfing down my breakfast. Fido managed somehow to get up on the bed without help and made a beeline for the tray. She grabbed the edge of it with her little paws, pulled herself up, and peeked over the edge at my food with big, hungry eyes. Her nose twitched overtime.

"You can't have any," I said with my mouth full.

She whimpered.

"You're a strict vegetarian."

She whimpered louder.

"Dad said no."

She gave me sad, pitiful eyes.

"Oh, all right, one bite, but don't let Dad find out."

I held out a smoky link and she snatched it and disappeared under the tray. I heard munching, then a tiny burp.

After I finished eating, I got dressed. I checked my look in the mirror over my dresser: plain, skinny boy in worn jeans and the T-shirt he slept in with scraggly brown hair, a small chin with a slight crease down the middle, a small nose that tilted up and showed too much nostril, and a neck that could stop growing any time without any complaint from me. Final grade: U (for Unsatisfactory).

Fido jumped down from the bed and ran to her cage to relieve herself. I took the opportunity to lock her in. She rushed to the bars and started to screech.

"Quiet," I said, and gave her the Stony Stare. She shut up. Which was a little cool.

"Sit," I said, just for fun.

She sat. Which was also a little cool. Still, a little cool for a dorky rodent with a mohawk was still almost totally uncool compared to any dog, even a toy poodle.

"If you want to make any noise while I'm gone, Dad will kick you out on your tailless behind. And there are a lot of cats in our neighborhood, so . . ."

I stopped and thought about this, then added, "So go ahead and make as much noise as you want."

I left the room and closed the door behind me.

Dad was in the kitchen washing dishes. He was wearing his WHAT PART OF "IT'S NOT READY YET" DO YOU NOT UNDERSTAND? apron.

"You didn't leave your dishes in your room,

did you?" he asked. "This is exactly why we don't allow you—"

"Sorry," I said, and ran back to my room.

Fido jumped up and down when I came through the door. I grabbed the tray.

"I just forgot this," I said to her, and turned to leave.

She screeched.

"Quiet," I commanded.

She shut up.

"Good pig," I said.

"Is that creature going to screech all day?" Dad asked when I returned to the kitchen. "I have an enormous amount of work to do."

I shrugged. "Ask Mom. She's the guinea pig expert."

"If it keeps it up, I will not hesitate to return the infernal creature to the pet shop posthaste," Dad said.

"Copy that," I said.

He glared at me.

Old habits die hard. "I mean fine, wonderful, sounds great."

I grabbed my backpack and my hoodie

and headed for the front door. I heard Fido screeching upstairs before I was outside. On the porch, I turned and saw Dad through the kitchen window, holding his ears.

Hmm, I thought, grinning ear to ear, *maybe he should have gotten me a dog after all.*

4. My best friend's dog was perfection.

He was a black Lab, tall, sleek, fast, strong, and beautiful. Buddy did all the cool dog things: he heeled, spoke, rolled over, played dead, ran alongside Murphy's bike, caught things in midair, and lots more. He was the best dog in Rustbury. Everybody in town loved Buddy.

Everybody but Dad.

Murphy and Buddy were playing in their front yard when I walked up. Murph threw a dirty green tennis ball, and Buddy jumped up and caught it and brought it back to him. Buddy wouldn't let go of it, so Murph had to try to pull it out of his big, sharp white teeth. Buddy was snarling. His lips were curled up and you could see his gums. What a dog! Murph was so lucky.

And then there was me. My plan was to keep Fido a secret, even from Murph. It wouldn't be easy, but, hopefully, she'd keep screeching and Dad would take her back. Problem over. So I would have to keep the secret for only a little while.

"Hey, Smurph," I said. Smurph was Murph's nickname when he was little. He doesn't want to be called it anymore, but he lets me, because we go way back, and because I promised I'd never say it when there was anyone else around.

"'Sup, Roof?" he said, and let go of the ball. Buddy dropped it and galloped away with his tongue hanging out. I was jealous.

"Nothing," I said with a shrug. "'Sup with you?"

He shrugged. We shrugged a lot lately. "I guess A.G.'s sick."

A.G. was Murph's little sister. She was six and there was always something wrong with her. She got hurt a lot and got sick even more. Even when she wasn't hurt or sick, something was always bothering her. Like she was always itchy or hot or achy or something was in her eye or she was freaked out by something, like an ant. Okay, I didn't have a dog, but at least I didn't have a sister.

"So she's not coming with us?"

"She's staying home."

We both smiled and said, "Sweet!" at the same time.

Then we said, "Jinx!" at the same time.

Then we said, "Idaho Jinx!" Which made us even.

"Did you hear about the poisonous ducks at the lake?" Murph asked.

This was pretty classic Murph. Murph liked fooling around.

"Nope," I said, playing along. "I didn't hear about that, Smurph."

"Really? Everybody's talking about it."

"So these ducks are poisonous, huh?"

"Totally."

You had to be careful with Murph. Sometimes when he said weird stuff like this he was actually telling the truth. He definitely liked to mess around with your head. Test you. See if he could possibly fool you.

Once he swore polar bears had black skin and see-through fur. *"Translucent* fur" is what he actually said. (He has a pretty amazing vocab, which is both cool and uncool.) I didn't believe him, so he showed me a bunch of animal Web sites that said polar bears are black with translucent fur. He even showed me a book that said it.

So I had to be careful. Poisonous ducks sounded pretty crazy, but so did black polar bears. Face it, the world's full of crazy stuff.

"So how do these poisonous ducks . . . uh . . . you know . . . ?"

"Administer their venom?" he said.

There was that vocab again.

"Right," I said.

"Via their feathers."

"They run around stabbing people with their feathers?"

"No, dude. Ducks don't attack. It's a *defense* mechanism."

"So what attacks ducks? Besides duck

hunters, I mean. How do the ducks defend themselves against guns, by the way?"

"They can't, lucky for us. But not just humans prey on them. There are coyotes, hawks, foxes—even dogs. Once a predator gets pricked by the feathers, it's toast."

I looked at Buddy sprinting across the neighbors' lawns. For a couple of seconds, I felt prickles of fear on the back of my neck. Then I remembered how Murph makes stuff up.

"I've been keeping Buddy away from the lake till the parks-and-rec guys take care of the problem," he said.

"What will they do?"

"Capture and destroy."

"That's harsh."

"You wouldn't say that if you had a dog."

I gave him the Stony Stare. That was a low blow, and he knew it.

"Sorry, dude. Look, let me put Buddy inside, then we can stop at the lake on the way to school and I'll show you the ducks."

I looked at my watch. "We're going to be late as it is. Dad was giving me a hard time about—"

Oops.

"About what?"

"The Dump," I said, then switched subjects. "The lake isn't on the way to school, dude."

"We could ride our skateboards. Then we'd definitely have time to check out the ducks and maybe even get to school on time."

"I don't have my board with me, Murph."

"Then ride my bike. Yeah, you can *tow* me. That'll be totally faster!"

He called Buddy, and he returned immediately. What a dog! Murph put him in the house, then got his board and his bike from the garage, and we rode toward the lake, me pedaling and him holding on.

"I don't believe you, by the way, about this poisonous duck business!" I yelled back at him over the noise of our wheels.

"Well then, I'll have to prove it to you, won't I?" he yelled back, grinning.

5. "No way are those ducks poisonous."

The ride was over. We were at the lake. Murph was pointing at some ducks swimming out on the greenish water.

"Those are mallards."

"They *look* like mallards, don't they," Murphy said, chuckling to himself. Then suddenly he turned and looked at me, his face completely serious. "Trust me, pal. They're not mallards."

"How do you know?"

"I know. I could prove it to you, but then we'd be late for school."

I checked my watch. "We're gonna be late anyway." I squinted at him. He gave me his poker face. It was the moment of truth. Or lies. "Show me," I said, stupidly.

There's one born every minute.

"This way," he said.

He led me down a path, and all of a sudden, a whole bunch of squawking crows flew up out of some reeds. I about had a heart attack, but Murph stayed real cool, like he knew it was going to happen, which he probably did somehow. He parted the reeds with his arms.

"Voilà!" he said. "Observe one of the victims of *Anas tossicus*, aka the poisonous duck."

He grinned a smirky, gloaty grin.

I looked where he wanted me to look, and saw what he wanted me to see, and it totally creeped me out. *Freaked* me out. I thought I might puke.

It was a fox. A dead one, frozen stiff, lying on its back in the reeds, its paws frozen in the air, like it died fighting off something. Its eyes looked scared. There was a big black hole in its furry white belly. I was pretty sure the black stuff was dried blood.

I looked out at the ducks. *Fox ate a duck,* I thought. *Fox got poisoned. Fox died. Little animals are feeding on Fox's guts, hence spreading the poison all around* . . .

I looked back at Murphy, and he totally busted a gut. I don't mean like the fox's busted gut. I mean, he just completely lost it. He laughed himself boneless, fell on the ground laughing, laughed himself silly.

Why? Because he got me again, got me big-time.

"I *so* got you," he said, holding his sides.

My best friend is one seriously crazy and clever dude.

"We're *so* late," I said.

🐾 🐾 🐾

Twelve minutes late, to be exact.

"Why, hello again, Murphy," Tamra, the secretary, said.

That's right: Hello, *Murphy*. Like I wasn't there.

She slid two tardy slips across the counter. "So what's the story this time, Mr. Molloy?"

"Poisonous ducks at the lake," Murph said with a sly grin.

Tamra beamed. "Get to class, you scamp!"

She didn't bother asking me what my story was.

We filled out our slips, slid them back across the counter, then headed toward our classroom. I walked faster than Murph. Unlike him, I cared about being late. This made him laugh.

"Chillax. We have our tardy slips. We can't be *double* tardy."

I slowed down. A little.

It was kind of amazing to me. Murph never cared if he missed announcements or the pledge or classwork or anything. And even though he was always late and fooling around, he always got along with everybody: teachers, kids, even girls. Everybody liked Murphy.

It had been like that as long as I could remember, since way back in kindergarten, where we met. I doubt I noticed back then how liked he was, because, you know, kindergartners can't really *think* at their age, but I just kind of knew that he was different. It wasn't only that he had this really big ole smile and this jack-o'-lantern mouth and these crazy curls all over his head, and that he never stopped moving or laughing and giving off this, like, *hum* of fun. It was mostly that he was so totally, immediately, completely *likable*.

So I did whatever it took to be his friend, which didn't turn out to be very much. With Murph, if you wanted to be his friend, you were. "The more the merrier!" he liked to say, even way back in kindergarten.

When we finally reached our room, I saw Dmitri Sull flash Murph a thumbs-up. Murph didn't notice because he was playing the room: taking bows, mugging, clowning, pretending to choke and trip, checking his wrist (he doesn't own a watch, of course—why would he?). All eyes were on him, and his were on no one in particular.

Feeling snubbed, Dmitri glared at me, then, slowly and dramatically, turned his fist to a thumbs-down. If Murph was my best friend, Dmitri was my worst. We were friends only because we were both Murph's friends. The more the merrier.

Murph handed our teacher, Ms. Charp, his tardy slip like it was a message from the emperor. I handed her mine like it was a murder confession. She said to me behind her hand (for the umpteenth time), "You might consider walking alone to school, Rufus."

I shrugged and slipped away. No eyes were on me, thank Dog.

"That's right: *poisonous* ducks," Murph was saying. "At the lake. And I can prove it. Ask Rufus. He saw them."

I looked up from the floor to find he was pointing at me.

"Tell 'em, Roof!"

I was so disoriented, I collided with Lurena Shraits's desk. Then Linus Axelbrig's. Finally, I found my own and sat in it. Dmitri slapped my elbow. He sat next to me. Fabulous.

"So you saw these 'poisonous ducks,' huh?" he said.

He was leaning uncomfortably close to me, his sharp nose and sharp chin closing together like a lobster's claw. Okay, not really. We'd been working on similes in language arts, and sometimes I go a little too far. But he does have really pointy features.

I looked back at Murph. He and his audience were already on to something else. No one was looking at me anymore. My moment of fame and glory had come and gone, and I'd spent it tripping over desks.

"Did you see them or not?" Dmitri hissed, and slapped my elbow again.

I found his nagging and slapping irritating. Being late was irritating, too. Being tricked by Murphy was irritating. Mom getting me a guinea pig instead of a dog was irritating. The guinea pig herself was irritating. Dad was irritating. Life was irritating.

So when Dmitri slapped my elbow for the third time, I snarled at him and flashed him my teeth. I have pretty pointy canines.

He whispered, *"Whoa! Weirdopath!"* then inched his desk away.

Dmitri moved to Rustbury just before school started this year. From day one, he acted like he'd lived here all his life. He teased and bullied guys the second he met them. He was always bragging about all the great things he used to do back in Irondale, which, of course, was a zillion times better than Rustbury. His parents obviously had tons of money because he always got every cool electronic thing right when it came out and always wore brand-new athletic shoes and jeans and hoodies and caps, which always had the right logos and designs and brand names on them.

He also had a dog, a black chow named Mars. Mars was scary (he bit kids a lot) and too poofy for my tastes (his coat looked kind of like a cross between a lion's and a standard poodle's, between clippings), but he was still a big black dog—and not a small orange guinea pig with a mohawk.

At least Fido wasn't poofy, though. If there's anything I hate, it's a poofy pet.

Yet somehow none of this—the cool stuff, the teasing, bullying, and bragging, the vicious black chow—made Dmitri popular, which was my theory of what he wanted most. Popularity was the reason he stalked Murphy all the time. He probably believed that being friends with

Murph would make him as popular as Murph, or that Murph's likability would rub off on him. Neither of these things came true. A lot of kids just ignored him. The ones he teased and bullied dreaded him. I was in this second group.

Because I was Murph's best friend, I ended up getting stuck with Dmitri a lot, which would be fun only if I loved getting put down and laughed at a lot, which I don't. It's like Dmitri was on some campaign to prove to Murph that I was the worst choice ever for best friend and that he was a much better candidate. Luckily—so far, anyway—Murph didn't seem to be buying it, or even paying much attention. That was one good thing about Murph: he only added friends; he didn't subtract. It was also one bad thing about him.

Finally, Ms. Charp regained control of her classroom and convinced Murph to take his seat, which was between Shireen and Kiesha, two of the nicest girls in class. They both smiled at him. I stared at the three of them for a while, then peeked over at Dmitri, who was looking at them, too. He stopped and peeked at me when I stopped and peeked at him, then we both quickly looked away and tried to act cool. True, he and I didn't have much in common, but one thing we did have was that we both wished we were Murph.

6. School flew by that day, just to make me mad.

Wasn't that always the way? If something supercool was going to happen after school, time moved like a glacier, but when something even worse than school was waiting for you— *WHAM!*—your teacher was sick and you got some pushover sub, or there was a field trip. That day we had Marketplace. Marketplace is noisy and crazy and it sure beats regular school, but it was the last thing I wanted that particular day. I wanted a long, slow, dull day. Figures.

For Marketplace, everyone brings in stuff to sell and then sets up booths to trade "goods and services" with one another. The goods could be old toys or games or stuff, or they could be art projects or handmade jewelry or baked goods—

you know, real quality items. The services could be something like painting faces or fingernails, or reading palms or guessing people's weight. Of course, we don't use real money. We use school money, which is essentially play money. Counterfeit cash. Totally worthless outside of school.

I hadn't remembered about Marketplace, so I didn't have anything to sell. I thought quick and decided to mix up kids' full names into something funny using old Scrabble tiles. (I buy old sets online for next to nothing; it's kind of a hobby and is definitely not worth going into right now.) After I anagrammed the names, I glued them onto wooden paint stirrers my mom brought home from work. (This is part of the hobby, but again, it's not worth going into detail about now. . . .) I charged one fake school buck each.

This was exactly what I did last Marketplace, so I still had tiles and stirrers I never got around to taking home in my locker. I didn't exactly have a line of customers out the door. Murphy came by (MURPHY MOLLOY = ROY

HOLLYMUMP), and Dmitri Sull (SIR DULL TIM), and Linus Axelbrig (BRAILLE SIXGUN), and Lurena Shraits (ARTHURLESS ANI, though she said she preferred her own RUTHLESS NAIRA; she's kind of an anagram freak herself).

Murph did magic tricks. He knew all kinds—cards, rope, coins, balls and cups, you name it—and had been doing them for years. He liked knowing how to do things that grabbed people's attention. He called himself the Amazing Roy Hollymump (he used the stirrer as a sign) and had a long line all day. He would have gathered up everybody's money if he didn't close up shop so often and go and blow his earnings at other booths. I mean, how many times did a dude really need his palm read in a single day? Especially by some ten-year-old girl (Shireen) who can't even spell? *I'm* the one who can spell! Me and Lurena—the anagram freaks.

Of course, Murph spent money at my booth, too, and did tip pretty generously....

So anyway, before I even knew what was happening, the final bell rang. It was 3:35. The school day was over. I had to go home. To Dad. And to Fido.

Wasn't there a little more long division we could do?

I actually asked Ms. Charp if she needed any help around the classroom after school, and said that I'd be happy to stay to make up for being late. I suggested sweeping up stray phony money and other trash from Marketplace, or maybe clapping whiteboard erasers together.

"This guy just can't get enough education, Ms. Charp!" Murph laughed, grabbing me by the belt. "I'll be sure to get him back bright and early tomorrow!"

"On time would be nice, Mr. Molloy," Ms. Charp said as Murph dragged me out the door and into the hall.

"So what did Shireen predict?" I asked.

"Shireen?"

"She read your palm."

"Oh, that. She said we'll be late for school every day this week."

"Why did you have to go back so many times to hear that?"

"Because of the way she blushes when she holds my hand." He pretended to be in love. Yuck.

"Did you get your future told?" he asked.

"No, but I did buy this sandwich bag filled with dog biscuits."

"You don't have a dog, Roof."

I squinted at him. "Thanks for reminding me. They're for Buddy. Can I feed them to him, though?"

"Sure. Let's go."

"My dad said I had to come straight home from school today."

"But you just volunteered to stay late and help Ms. Charp."

"Yeah, I did, didn't I? Why would I do that?"

I was biding time, trying to think of a way to get my big foot out of my mouth. I wanted to come clean, *My mom bought me a guinea pig instead of a dog—can you BELIEVE that?—and I gotta go home and relieve my dad from taking care of her, but I don't really want to; in fact, I don't want to so bad that I volunteered to stay late at school.*

Instead, I said, "Sometimes staying after school with Ms. Charp is better than going home to my dad."

Sadly enough, Murph bought this hook, line, and sinker.

You see, Murph's dad was cool, like Buddy, and Murph's mom. She would never bring Murph home a guinea pig if what he really wanted was a dog. No way. His parents were normal people who acted normal and understood why boys wanted normal things like dogs. They weren't like my parents at all.

"I'll come with you to your house then," Murph said.

"No!" I said way too urgently.

"What is the matter with you, dude?"

"On second thought, you take the biscuits and give them to Buddy. I'll go home alone. I . . . I . . . I always end up *late* when I hang out with you."

"You gotta point there," Murph said.

"By chance are you talking about the top of Roof's head?" said Dmitri, walking up behind me.

"My head isn't pointed," I said.

"Oh, that's right, I forgot," Dmitri said. "It's *dull*."

He looked to Murph for a reaction, but Murph was busy making goofy faces at Shireen, who was walking across the street with Kiesha. Dmitri was annoyed that Murphy had missed his wisecrack.

"I said Rufus's head isn't pointy, Murph— it's dull," Dmitri said again. "You get it? Dull, not pointy?"

Murphy walked away without noticing Dmitri had spoken to him. Dmitri sighed and hustled after him. Murph caught up to Shireen and started talking fast and making wild gestures with his hands. Shireen and Kiesha laughed. Dmitri tried to butt in, but Murph squeezed him out. He doesn't like to be interrupted while performing.

I was beginning to wonder if my best friend was outgrowing me, outcooling me, out*everything*ing me.

"Bye, Murph," I said to myself, and walked away toward home and my uncool dad and my tiny, mock, uncool dog.

7. I heard the howling a block away.

Okay, maybe not howling. It was too screechy for howling. But I read once that grasshopper mice howl, and if a little mouse like that can do it, why not a guinea pig?

I took my time walking that last block, because, one, I wanted Dad to be punished for as long as possible for refusing to get me a dog, and, two, I knew he was going to try to make it seem like it was my fault that he was stuck with a guinea pig all day when it absolutely was not. A part of me hoped he didn't get any work done at all because of Fido's screeching, and that his nerves were shot, and that, consequently, he would tell me the second I stepped through the door that he would be immediately returning the rodent to its place of purchase for a full refund. That part of me, by the way, was the largest part. All that was left was this little tiny part that was afraid of him and an even tinier part that felt sort of bad for him. I ignored these parts, though, because he so deserved every bad thing that happened to him for not being a normal dad who liked dogs.

So I didn't want to get home because I wanted Dad to suffer, but I *did* want to get home so I could see him all wigged out and frazzled, though I *didn't* want him getting all wigged out and frazzled on *me*. My big fantasy was that I'd walk through the door and he'd be running around the house pulling out what was left of his hair, yelling, "YOU CAN HAVE A DOG! YOU CAN HAVE A DOG! JUST GET RID OF THE *GUINEA PIG*!"

Our house is on a cul-de-sac with three other houses that look pretty much like it: two stories, big windows in front, gray shutters that don't shut, green aluminum siding, two-car garage, steep driveway, baby trees in the yard, and a store-bought sign that read:

**SOLICITORS
WILL BE
PROSECUTED
TO THE FULL
EXTENT OF
THE LAW.**

This was Dad's doing. On the front door he hung a sign he made with his computer:

There is no doorbell.
Do not knock.
To speak to residents,
enter the security code,
then press #.
If you do not know the
security code, please
turn around and
vacate the property.

Under the sign was a number keypad.

On the porch was a rubber welcome mat that read:

We're Glad You're Here!

This was Mom's attempt to warm up the fortress. She bought it at work.

I pressed the four button four times (the golf e-zine Dad works for is called *Fore!*), then the pound sign; I heard the clearance beep, and pushed the door open. A scowling man in a gray suit and fuzzy blue slippers was standing behind it. I jumped.

"H-Hi, Dad," I said as I stepped in and closed the door behind me.

The foyer we stood in was plunged into near darkness. The only light came from Dad's angry eyes.

"Hello, son," he said in a slow, sinister voice. It gave me chills. "How was school? Fine?"

I shrugged. "I guess."

"So glad to hear that."

My eyes began to adjust to the dark. I could see Dad smiling in this creepy way.

He has pointy canines, too. He looked pretty vampirelike.

Fido was still screeching, though it sounded quieter inside the house for some reason.

"Fido missed you today, I think," Dad said. "She's been calling for you. She's been calling for you *all day*. Ever since you left this morning, in fact. She's been calling for you, nonstop, all day, ever since early this morning when you left, Rufus." Then he let out a little, maniacal, "Heh-heh-heh-heh-heh."

"I'll g-go up and see what I can d-do," I said, and tried to squeeze by him.

He took a step sideways, blocking me.

"Not *up*, son," he whispered. "Out."

"Out?"

He turned and walked toward the kitchen in an undead, zombielike way. At the sink, he pointed out the window. His eyes were sort of twitching and winking. I got up on my tiptoes and looked out.

He was pointing at my tree house. I'd kind of forgotten it was there. It wasn't a homemade tree house. It was a store-bought tree house, made of giant, fat, interlocking, colorful plastic pieces, like the kind little kids' backyard play sets were made of. Dad bought it to avoid all the noise and mess of hammering and sawing.

"Is that where Fido is?" I asked.

He nodded.

"Because she was too loud?"

He nodded again.

That was why I heard her so far away, I thought.

"I'll go out and try to quiet her down."

"Yes," Dad said. "Do."

I backed away from him. He didn't move a muscle, except the ones in his eyes. They (the eyes) followed me as I backed away. They didn't blink. I wondered if it was possible that Fido the guinea pig had driven my dad out of his mind in one single day. To be fair, since he started working at home, it wasn't like she had all that far to drive him.

"Are we going to have to take her back to the pet store?" I asked, hoping I wasn't overplaying my hand. I wanted him to think it was his decision, *his* idea.

"We will discuss that with your mother when she returns from work," he said, still not blinking.

"Copy that," I said. Oops.

He squinted at me.

"I mean, that sounds good, Dad," I said with a put-on smile. "Discussing it with Mom after work sounds excellent. Can't wait."

Then I ran out of the house.

8. Fido was in my tree house.

She was in her cage. It was covered with a quilt, probably to muffle her screeches. Dad had stacked books on the quilt so that Fido couldn't drag the quilt off. I imagined Dad carrying first Fido and the cage up the tree, then the quilt, then the books, the whole time furious that he wasn't at his desk, editing. I wondered who he was the maddest at: Fido, Mom, or me. He should have been maddest at himself, of course. But I've already gone into that. . . .

When I pulled the quilt off, Fido squealed. Like a pig. I guess that's why they call them that. Then she gripped the bars and whined and panted and wagged her butt.

"Quiet!" I said, to show her who was the boss, and she pulled her act together. I don't mind saying it: I kind of enjoyed how obedient she was. It was fun telling someone else what to do for a change.

I wondered if I should open the cage door. The tree house had no real doors or windows. If she wanted to escape and could climb (I didn't know anything about the species then), she might shinny down the tree and be gone. If she couldn't climb, she might fall out of the tree and be badly injured, even killed.

I opened the cage door.

She ran out, but did not try to escape. Instead, she darted up my pant leg to my T-shirt, up my T-shirt to my face, and licked my chin. She could climb all right.

I pinched the back of her furry little neck and lifted her up. She hung there, limp and whimpering, her tiny, pink, creepy, clawed feet twitching. Her eyes were big and set on either side of her head, which made her snout look huge. The snout had a vertical white stripe running down it. This beast didn't look anything like a dog.

She didn't look like a rat, either, though, or

a pig, for that matter. She looked like some sort of alien life-form. Where was Guinea anyway?

I felt bad after a couple of seconds of holding her by her scruff, so I set her down in my lap. She started straight for my chin again.

"Down!" I said.

She froze, then returned to my lap.

"Sit!" I added.

She sat.

I wondered if maybe they sold trained guinea pigs at that pet store of Mom's. If that was true, Dad could silence Fido anytime he wanted to. Which meant Fido wouldn't drive him crazy anymore, and we wouldn't have to take her back. All I had to do was tell Dad that when Fido was noisy, he should say, "Quiet!"

So I didn't tell him that.

Who knows. Maybe Fido wouldn't have listened to him anyway. Maybe she only listened to me.

I carried the cage down out of the tree house and set it on the grass. Fido climbed down out of the tree on her own. She could have bolted easy, but she ran in circles around me, her tongue flapping out of her mouth, her butt wagging. I think she wanted to play.

I picked up a twig and tossed it.

"Fetch!" I said.

She shot after it, her plump body galloping through the grass. She returned with the twig held tightly in her long rodent front teeth. Her nose twitched like crazy. I took the twig.

"Good pig," I said very quietly, and gave her a tiny scratch on her head.

She rolled over and exposed her belly.

🐾 🐾 🐾

The meeting was held in the Conference Room. Yes, we have a Conference Room at home. Dad feels it's necessary. Mom calls it the Family Gathering Room, but she never fools anyone. It's a small room, just big enough for a small wooden table and three chairs. The walls, like all the walls in our house, are wallpapered. After work, Mom doesn't like thinking about or seeing paint. The wallpaper in the Conference/Family Gathering Room had a harvest theme: haystacks, pumpkins, and barns. (The wallpaper in my room, by the way, has a race car motif. *Vroom vroom.* Pretty funny considering we own two hybrids.)

"The issue on the floor is the guinea pig," Dad said. "I make a motion we return it to the pet store. Do I hear a second?"

"Wait a second, Art . . . ," Mom said.

"I have a second," Dad said.

"I said, WAIT a second. Can't we discuss this first?"

Dad sighed.

Believe it or not, I was relieved at Mom's interruption. I mean, before I came through the door from school, I would have seconded Dad's motion in a nanosecond. But suddenly I wasn't so sure. Why? I don't know, really. I still wanted a dog—and Fido definitely was not a dog—but playing Fetch with Fido had been sort of interesting, if not exactly fun. Was there some way to keep Fido *and* get a dog? Probably not. But I wasn't as eager to get rid of her as I had been just a couple of hours ago.

"Fine," Dad said. "The floor is open for discussion. Discuss, Raquel. Discuss."

"I don't think we've given Emmeline much of a chance to adapt to her new home."

"Fido," I said.

"Right. Fido. Sorry. I don't think we should make any decisions until she's had a chance to get to know us and we've had a chance to get to know her."

Very dramatically, Dad pulled a shoe out of hiding and slammed it onto the table—*WHAM!* Mom and I jumped. The shoe was one of Dad's shiny black leather jobs with laces and fringe. The laces and fringe were noticeably gnawed, and there were teeth marks on the tongue. Dad glared at Mom, then at me.

"What?" I said. "Why are you looking at me?"

"End of discussion," Dad announced through gritted teeth. "Return the rodent, Raquel."

Suddenly I wondered, *Was I losing my mind, too?* No way was I going to change sides, not after all I been through in my fight for dog ownership. A little freaky fun with a furball was not enough for me to put an end to my dreams. I wanted a dog, not a trained rat.

"I second your motion, Dad," I said.

"Good," Dad said. "All in favor? Aye."

"Aye," I said.

"The ayes have it," he said.

"Then I guess I'll take her back," Mom said, with sobs in her throat and tears in her eyes.

I didn't like watching her cry, so I stared at the haystacks and barns.

9. How does a whole pet store disappear?

That's what we all wanted to know as we stared in through the dark plate-glass windows of the empty retail space Mom claimed was the pet store called Petopia the day before.

"You're sure we're in the right place?" Dad asked. "These strip malls all look alike."

"Yes," Mom said. "It's right next door to Rufus's old preschool, just like I said it was."

She pointed to the Mudpie Institute, which I remembered more from driving by and Mom saying, "Look, Rufus, there's where you went to preschool!" than from actually going there.

"Isn't there a sign saying where they moved to?" Dad asked.

There wasn't. There wasn't a sign of any

kind at all. If they'd moved, they had taken everything with them and left no note saying where they went.

"Is there a phone number on the receipt?" Dad asked.

Mom gulped. "I can't find the receipt. I don't think I kept it. I didn't think we'd be needing it."

"I'll call the Better Business Bureau!" Dad said. He was getting worked up. "I'll call the police! This is a scam! A fraud! There has to be a way to return this unwanted merchandise!"

"Try to relax, Art," Mom said with a nervous smile. "You have the whole day tomorrow to find them."

"Just because I work *at home* does not mean I have the whole day *free*, Raquel," Dad said. This was a sore spot with him.

"I didn't mean—" Mom started to say.

"I will look it up when we get home," Dad said. "And I'll find it, too." And he marched off to the car, climbed in, slammed the door, and started the engine.

Mom and I hustled over and got in. Fido was in the backseat in her cage. She began to whine.

"Silence the animal," Dad said.

I leaned over the cage and whispered, *"Quiet."* She stopped whining.

Dad whipped his head around. "What just happened?"

"What?" I was playing innocent.

"Why did she stop?"

"I don't know. I guess she heard you?"

Dad straightened up a bit. "Yeah?" he said, proudly.

"I think Emmeline respects you, Art," Mom said.

"Fido, Raquel."

"Sorry," Mom said. "Fido."

🐾 🐾 🐾

Petopia was not in the phone book, which was weird, and we couldn't find it online. It was as if the place never existed. Or Mom had the name wrong. Dad insisted she study the other pet stores in the phone book very carefully.

"Obviously, you've made some mental error," he said. "All pet stores list themselves in the white pages and usually take out an ad in the yellow pages. They *want* people to find them. You are simply remembering the name wrong."

"No, I'm remembering it right," Mom said. "I don't think they had been there very long. Maybe they'll be in the next phone book. Of course, that won't help, will it?" She smiled.

Dad fumed. "We need to find the receipt, Raquel."

We turned the house upside down but couldn't find it.

"How about we abandon her in the woods?" Dad suggested later in the Conference Room.

"That's not funny," Mom said.

"I'm not entirely sure I'm not entirely serious."

"I can easily find a home for Fido," Mom said. "There must be lots of kids who would love to have a guinea pig."

"I suppose we'll be *giving* her away then," Dad said. "No refund."

"We could try to sell her, Art, but it could take a while. . . ."

"At this point, I'm willing to *pay* someone to take her."

"Art, we've only had her a day. . . ."

"After she's gone, can I get a real dog?" I asked before I could stop myself. I had promised myself I wouldn't bring the dog issue up till Fido was history.

Dad gave me the Stony Stare.

"Not now," Mom whispered to me. "Your dad's upset."

"No dog," Dad said. "What more proof need we that animals do not belong in this house than what we saw today? And this was just a *rodent!* Imagine a *canine!* Find yourself another hobby, Rufus. Collect something. Cards. Stamps. Shells."

"I already collect something. I collect Scrabble tiles."

Dad's eyebrows rose. "Fine. Good. That's a nice, quiet hobby. Keep it up. And good for the mind, too. And no fleas. And it doesn't need to be walked. And—"

I wasn't in the mood for the list. I never was, actually. So I interrupted.

"No, you're right, Dad. Scrabble tiles make a great hobby. But they're not exactly a *pet*, are they? Technically, to be a pet, they'd have to be *alive*, wouldn't they? And they aren't, are they?"

Dad smirked. "No dog, Rufus. Ever. Meeting adjourned." And he left the Conference Room.

"Just be patient, sunshine," Mom said with a sympathetic smile. "It will all work out somehow."

"Yeah. I'll grow up, move out, get my own place, and then I'll get a dog. In the meantime, I'll make do with a bunch of little wooden tiles with letters and numbers on them. I can spell out *Labrador retriever* even if I can't ever have one. At least I think I can. I can spell *Lab* anyway."

"It won't take that long." Mom laughed.

"No? How do you know?"

"I don't know how I know. I just know."

"Do you know Dad?"

She smiled. "Yes. Somewhat."

"Did you hear what he just said?"

"Give him time."

"I'm in fifth grade, Mom. I've given him plenty of time. I'd like a dog while I'm still young enough to enjoy one."

She laughed. What is it about my tragedies that she finds so hilarious?

"I'll work on him," she said. "He's only been working at home a few months. He hasn't been as productive as he hoped he would be. He thought he'd get more work done at home than he did when he worked at the office, but that hasn't been the case, and he blames everything but himself for it." She stopped to sigh. "He'll work it out and our lives will go back to normal again."

I blinked at her. I blinked again. Then I said, "*Normal?* When has the guy ever been *NORMAL*?"

"Raquel, Rufus," Dad said, returning to the room holding a plastic fork, "I just spotted this in the garbage. Do you two need a refresher on what plastic items are recyclable?"

Mom and I looked at each other and laughed.

10. *"Eeeee!"* I squealed when I opened my backpack.

Fido poked her head out and licked my nose. It was the next morning and I was at my locker. How did she get into my backpack? I can't say for sure, but here's my theory:

1. She slept at the foot of my bed.
2. I slept through my alarm.
3. Dad knocked and said, "You slept through your alarm. Get moving or you'll be late."
4. I got up, pulled on some cleanish clothes, and ran out the door.
5. Downstairs, Dad said I had to:
    a. Eat something.
    b. Brush my teeth.
    c. Put Fido in the tree house and cover her with the quilt.

6. I ate a banana and threw the peel in the compost, not the garbage.
7. I got my toothbrush wet.
8. I carried Fido in her cage out to the tree house.
9. I set my backpack down to spread the quilt.
10. Fido opened the cage door that I probably didn't lock.
11. She crawled into my backpack that I probably didn't zip.
12. I ran to school without knowing I had a stowaway. (Note: I did not stop at Murph's.)
13. At my locker, I opened my backpack (it wasn't zipped) and . . . well, this is where I started.

So that was probably how Fido got to school. The big question, though, was: how was I going to keep anybody from finding out there was a guinea pig in my backpack?

"What's the dealio, Roof?" Dmitri said, slapping me too hard on the back. It was a good thing my backpack—with Fido in it—was in my locker at the time. Or was it?

I shoved Fido down into the bag and slammed my locker shut in one panicky motion, then squeaked, "H-Huh?"

"Whatcha hiding, Roof?" Dmitri said.

I shrugged. "N-Nothing. I'm not hiding nothing. I mean, anything."

"Never mind, dude. You seen Murph?"

I shook my head.

"You're useless." He walked away.

Fido started screeching inside the locker, so I opened the door and hissed, *"Quiet, you!"* and she stopped. I peeked around to see if anyone had seen me do that, and it didn't look like anyone had, so I peeked inside my bag.

"Listen," I whispered to Fido, who twitched her whiskers up at me. *"You have to be absolutely silent all day today, okay? You can't make one sound, or else I am dead. You understand?"*

She stared at me with those big dopey eyes, and I slapped myself in the forehead, literally, because I couldn't believe I was pleading with a guinea pig.

I zipped up the bag, slung it over my shoulder, and started off to class. I had a pretty good feeling Fido would not stay quiet in my locker all day, so I didn't see what choice I had but to bring her with me. I wasn't allowed to bring my backpack into class, but I would have to cross that bridge when I came to it, wouldn't I?

"Good morning, Rufus," Ms. Charp said when I walked through the door. "I'm glad to see you're on time today. Is Murphy sick at home or something?"

"No," I said. "I walked by myself today." Adults are such smart alecks.

"I see," she said with a nod and an Are-we-learning-a-lesson-from-this? look.

I walked away. I didn't want to hang around, not with a rat in my backpack.

"Didn't you forget something, Rufus?" she asked from behind me.

I stopped and turned around. Yes, I had. I had forgotten to come up with an excuse for bringing my backpack into class.

"Forgotten something, Ms. Charp?" I asked, stalling for time.

She pointed toward my backpack with her eyes.

I stalled longer by pretending not to notice.

"Your backpack, Rufus," she said at last.

"Oh, my *backpack!*"

The chips were down, and, like usual, I was drawing a blank. I could never think of good, believable lies when I needed them. I wondered if there was a Web site to help with that, or a book—*Lying for Dumbheads* or something.

The bell rang. I love when that happens.

"Well, you'll have to put it away later," Ms. Charp said.

I walked away, smiling. Sometimes good stalling techniques can make up for poor lying skills. Maybe someday I'll write my own book: *The Complete Dork's Guide to Hemming and Hawing.*

I went to my seat and hung my backpack on my chair. With my lunch and Fido in it, the whole desk/chair combo started to tip back-ward, so I quickly sat down. Crisis averted.

Dmitri was sitting next to me. He was fidgety and kept eyeing the door.

"You didn't walk with Murph today?" he asked.

"Nope."

Dmitri lived too far away and in the wrong direction to walk to school with Murph. His mom drove him to school in her new Navigator. Or sometimes his dad drove him in his new Bravada.

"I want to show him my new phone," Dmitri said, sliding open a shiny yellow plastic device with a screen. It looked like something a diver would use. "It's a U-phone," he said.

I'd seen U-phones on TV commercials, but I'd never seen one in the flesh. On TV these really cool city people—mostly adults—talked on them, and played games, and IMed each other, and used the GPS, and shot movies, and shopped online, and other stuff, and this one guy was a deep-sea diver watching *Finding Nemo* underwater, which was totally funny and cool. Of course Dmitri had one. I tried not to let him see how much I wanted to see it.

But he saw. He slid it shut and dropped it into his pocket.

"You're not allowed to have phones in class," I said.

"He'll probably be late," he said.

"He *is* late," I said.

"Shut up."

"And you have a rewarding day of learning, too, Dmitri," I said.

Then I rested my chin on my hands on my desk and sighed all the air out of my body. It was 9:13 a.m., and it had already been a long day.

11. Here's why you should never keep a rodent in your backpack at school all day.

- It will pee.
- It will poop.
- It will pee again.
- It will poop again.
- The pee and poop will ruin whatever you keep in your backpack, especially your sack lunch.
- If anyone finds out it is in there, you will get busted and humiliated in front of everybody.
- Worrying about all this could give you a heart attack.

I had to figure out a way to get Fido out of the school.

I considered calling Dad and having him come and pick her up, but interrupting his work seemed worse than having a guinea pig at school. I considered acting sick and getting sent home, but I worried Fido might start making noise while I was in the nurse's office, especially if the nurse made me say "Ahhh!" or something and Fido thought she was hurting me. Too risky.

And then I had an idea that seemed like it just might work, which sounds incredible, I know. In fact, the biggest thing going against it was that I thought of it.

I carefully stood up, pulled on my backpack, and walked toward Ms. Charp's desk.

"Yes, Rufus?" she said, looking up. "What is it? I'm about to begin class."

"I have to"—I looked around, then leaned forward and whispered—"*go to the bathroom.*"

"Couldn't you have gone before the bell, Rufus?" Ms. Charp said, a bit sternly.

I shrugged. "I didn't have to then."

"Fine, okay. Take a pass, and please hurry."

I leaned closer. *"I don't think this will be a hurry kind of trip,"* I whispered.

She stiffened in her chair. "Well then, you had better get going, hadn't you?"

I nodded and walked away.

"Oh, and Rufus . . . ," she said.

I stopped and looked back, trying to hide my smugness. You see, I was hoping she would stop me.

"Why don't you—?"

"Hang up my backpack while I'm out?" I said. "Precisely what I was thinking." And off I went.

I grabbed a bathroom pass, but I passed the bathroom. I didn't need to go. (Lie #1.) I then passed my locker (Lie #2) and left the building through the east doors (Lie #3, considering that's what I intended to do all along). Once I was outside, however, I had come to the end of my brilliant plan. The plan was: pretend you're going to the bathroom but instead take

Fido out of the building. I didn't think about what to do with her after that. I saw then that I probably didn't have a bright future as a criminal mastermind.

I leaned back against the closed door, trying to stay out of sight of anyone inside or outside of the school, and that's when I noticed the little groundskeeping shed. It had some green bushes around it. *Eureka!* I thought, and my plan lurched ahead to Phase 2.

I looked from side to side, tried to imagine some cool spy music in my head, but was only able to bring up the theme to *Fairly OddParents*, then ran in a crouch across the grass to the shed. When I got there, I ditched my bag under a bush, whispered, *"Stay quiet!"* to Fido, who had started to screech, and then I took off running . . . when it hit me: *lunch!*

I went back, pulled the bag out from under the bush, unzipped it, removed my sack lunch and—good thinking here—my homework, whispered again, *"Stay quiet!"* to Fido, then zipped up the bag, tossed it back under the bush, and took off running again . . . when another thought hit me: *lunch!* This time, Fido's.

Again I went back, pulled the bag out from under the bush, and unzipped it. I opened my sack lunch, took out the turkey sandwich Dad made me, pulled out the lettuce, and dropped it into the backpack. Fido started chirping happily.

"Quiet! I mean it!" I hissed.

She got quiet.

I tossed the backpack back under the bush *again* and took off running *again* toward the building, and ran straight into Murph. *WHAM!*

"Whoa! Roof! What are *you* doing out here, dude?" he asked as we picked ourselves up off the ground.

"I . . . I . . ." *Thinking Fast for Numbskulls,* where were you?

"You're late?" he asked with a laugh. "Without me? I'm not sure that's okay with me."

"That's it!" I said. "I'm *late!* Late, late, late! Boy, am I late!"

He laughed. "Guess we better get in there and get our tardy slips then, Mr. Late Guy."

Oops. But I wasn't really late, in fact, was I? I'd already been to class, in fact, hadn't I? I had a bathroom pass, in fact, didn't I? Now I was really in a mess, in fact, wasn't I?

"No hurry," I said. "We're already late. We can't be *double* late!"

Murph laughed again. "Attaboy, Roof! That's the spirit. Still, not much to do out here, is there? Might as well get to class. Am I right?"

He was right. The thing to do was follow him. As long as I stuck with Murph, nothing bad could happen to me, because as long as I stuck with him, no one would pay any attention to me.

"Lead on, Mr. Molloy," I said.

For a guy who never came up with many bright ideas, I was coming up with an awful lot of them. Which worried me.

As I hoped, no one noticed me in the office when we picked up our tardy slips. (I jammed mine in my pocket.) And no one noticed me when we walked through the door to class—all eyes were on Murphy, as usual. I handed Ms. Charp back the bathroom pass, which, if he even noticed, Murph probably figured it was my tardy slip. Then I snuck away quietly to my seat. I was pretty darn proud of myself. All had gone according to plan. I had gotten myself out of a pretty sticky situation.

And into another one.

12. Recess is a joke.

The adults at school think it's their big gift to us, a time for us to go outdoors and relax and have fun with our friends. Yeah, right. Recess basically lasts the time it takes for a group of school kids to run outside, agree on something fun to do, get started doing it, then have to turn around and go back in. If you're going to have any fun, you've got to be smart, prepared, and organized. Here are some tips:

- Do the same activity every day. Less time wasted choosing.
- Pick an activity that requires little or no equipment. Less time spent gathering stuff.
- If it's a team activity like a sport or game— which, for guys, it usually is—pick teams

when time's not so crucial, like during class.

- Continue the same game the whole school week, so you can come close to kind of finishing maybe a quarter of one by Friday.

- Make everybody (except Murphy) swear to play every day; otherwise, it screws everything up. (You can't trust Murphy even if he does swear, so why bother? Some girl walks up and he's bye-bye.)

- Keep playing till one of the recess "teachers" (they're really just aides and kitchen ladies and stuff) comes over and tells you personally to go inside. You have earned those extra seconds. They are *yours*. Fight for them!

Anyway, me and some guys had planned a soccer game the day I hid Fido in the bush, so when the bell for recess rang, we stormed the ball field. We would have jumped right into it, but a couple of guys were out sick and they were on the same team. That meant some trading, which ate up a minute or two, which at recess is, like, an eon. Finally, the game started and we were all running around breathing fresh air and actually using our bodies when this little orange furball streaked across the field and everybody stopped and pointed and laughed and said, "What was *that*?"

It was Fido, of course.

Here's how she probably got loose:

• I forgot to zip my backpack.

It was pretty clear what she was doing out there, and it wasn't trying to kick a field goal. She was looking for yours truly. And she spotted him. And she made a beeline for him. And she was making some pretty good time as she cut a path across the field, let me tell you. I mean, the guys' mouths were all hanging open. Well, that's not so odd, but, believe me, they were amazed.

"It's a . . . guinea pig?" one of the brighter minds of my generation said.

"No, it's a woodchuck!" said one of the dimmer ones.

Once again, I was going to have to come up with some big, fat, believable lie or else, and Fido's surprising speed was rushing me, which I did not appreciate. It was no surprise that, in the end, I thought of nothing at all clever or helpful to do or say. I simply turned and ran away. This is my second main strategy—after stalling—when facing sticky situations: bolting.

Fido let out a bark. (Yeah, a bark. A teeny, tiny little bark, but it was a bark.) Then she kicked into high gear after me. That's right: She had a higher gear. It was ridiculous. The pet store must have been giving its rodents steroids.

I heard the guys behind me, laughing their heads off.

"Look at that fat rat go!" one screamed.

"It's following *Roof*!" one hollered.

I ran from the field to the basketball court, and the basketball-playing guys followed the soccer-playing guys, who followed Fido, who followed me, and I shouted, "Run, run, fast as you can! You can't catch me, I'm the . . ."

Where was the bell? It should have rung eons ago.

And through the playground I ran, and all the children stopped their play to watch, and smiled with glee, and they joined in the parade, and I scanned the skies for giant inflatable cartoon characters, but it was the wrong city, the wrong month, and the wrong parade for that. This was the First Annual Rustbury Spring Recess Parade, with Grand Marshal Fido, and starring Rufus the clown.

Finally, once every kid at school got a good look at my crazy, hyperspeed, punk guinea pig chasing me around the school grounds, the bell rang. I don't think anyone ever looked into it, but I'm pretty sure it was the longest fifteen-minute elementary-school recess in American history.

The bell had its usual effect. Everybody stopped what they were doing and started shuffling toward the building.

I seized the moment and ducked behind a bush. Fido followed me. I picked her up. She was panting heavily, but, overall, she seemed happy. She licked my face. I hissed and showed her my fangs. She whimpered.

"Back in the bag with you," I said.

I dashed from bush to bush till I was back at the one with my backpack under it. As I suspected, it was unzipped. Did I leave it that way, or did Fido know how to unzip? After all, she knew how to do a lot of really strange things.

I put her inside and zipped the bag shut.

"Stay!" I said.

She whined.

"Quiet!" I added.

She stopped whining.

I didn't trust that she wouldn't get out again somehow. I considered putting big rocks on the zippered end of the bag, but there weren't any big rocks handy. Wouldn't you know it? I thought I could lock the zippers together through the little holes in the zipper pulls, but I didn't have a lock. The backpack came with a little one with a tiny key, but who knows where that went. Then I got the brilliant idea to *tie* them together, but I didn't have anything to tie them with, until I looked down, and *duh*, I saw my shoes. I pulled the laces out of my left one and threaded it through the eyes of the zipper pulls and tied a good and tight knot. Then I put the bag under the bush and took a really deep breath because I hadn't breathed for a while. Then I ran back to class.

Murphy was entertaining everyone with a reenactment of the First Annual Rustbury Spring Recess Parade. He played me and used Shireen's poofy orange hat with the chin straps as Fido. He ran around the room dragging the hat behind him and everybody cracked up. When he saw me, he let go of Shireen's hat and went into this whole mock excited and honored routine, saying, "And *here* he is *nowwww* . . . Rufus! The boy who outran a . . . weird rodent thing! Put your hands together for him!"

Everybody snickered and clapped.

Then Ms. Charp walked in behind me, and they all knocked it off.

"Seats, please," she said, glaring at everyone. "I could hear you all the way from the staff lounge, for your information."

I slunk over to my desk. Dmitri scooted his desk over an inch. Lurena, in front of me, turned around.

"Of all the kids on the playground, why did she choose you, Rufus?" she asked.

I shrugged. "What makes you think it was a she?"

13. I wasn't as nervous to go home that day.

In fact, I couldn't wait to get there.

I slipped out after the bell without Murph seeing me, which isn't so tough to do; his focus is not usually on any one person unless it's a cute girl, which I am definitely not. Dmitri was helping out by trying desperately to show Murph his U-phone, which he had rushed to get from Ms. Charp before the bell had finished ringing. (The phone had beeped too many times during class and she had confiscated it.) I grabbed my jacket from my locker, scrambled outside, got my backpack from under the bush, and shot like a bullet toward home. My loose left shoe slowed me down, but I didn't stop to replace the lace, or to check on Fido in my bag. I didn't want anyone catching up with me and bugging me about the strange animal at recess. I just wanted to get home.

Dad was waiting for me just inside the door again.

"Hello, son," he said, his eyes glowing in the dark.

"Uh . . . hi, Dad."

"Fine day at school?"

"I guess."

I started to edge by him. He blocked me.

"Aren't you going to ask about *my* day?"

"Oh. Sure. How was your day, Dad?"

"On the whole, nerve-racking. Thanks for asking."

I looked at him blankly. "But Fido . . . ," I started to say, then wondered if I should volunteer how she stowed away and got loose at school and everything.

If Dad had a bad day, it couldn't have been Fido's fault. It must have been because of something else. I had taken off in a real rush this morning. I bet I forgot to do something, like bus my dishes. No, all I had was a banana. And I distinctly remembered throwing the peel in the compost, not the garbage. I couldn't think of anything I did or didn't do that would have made Dad's day "nerve-racking"—that is, anything that would have bugged him all day long.

"Why was it nerve-racking?" I asked.

"Well, first I spent over an hour hunting for your mother's Petopia," he said. "Without success, of course."

Good. That was Mom's fault.

"And then I spent the rest of the day trying to work while being driven stark-raving mad by the chattering of that ... that ..." His face got all red and scary. "That ... that ... *creature.*"

I took a couple of breaths, sort of letting his anger cloud blow over me. Then I said, "But Dad, Fido was—"

"So maybe you have some idea how we might rectify this untenable situation, son," he interrupted. "After all, I *do* have a living to make."

I shrugged. I wasn't exactly sure what he had said.

Luckily, Fido said something. I'd forgotten about her for a minute, if you can believe that.

That's what Dad can do to me. He can make me forget I have a chubby rat in a sack on my back.

When Fido started whining, Dad's shoulders shrank up to his ears.

"Find her, Rufus," he growled. "Find her wherever she is and I'll destroy her."

"But, *Dad*. She's right here, in my backpack. That's what I'm trying to tell you. She stowed away in it this morning somehow, and she's been at school with me all day."

Dad's shoulders fell. So did his jaw. And his face. I never saw somebody go from so tight to so loose so fast.

"But . . . ," he muttered.

"Look," I said, and I took off my backpack, untied the shoelace, and unzipped the zipper. A smell rushed out at my nostrils. It was not a nice smell. Right behind it was Fido's twitchy face. She, of course, licked mine. Well, my face wasn't twitchy. Then again, maybe it was.

"She was . . . ," Dad said, looking down at her. He was still acting weirdly dazed. "She was . . . with *you* . . . all day?"

"Yeah, she was in my backpack. After I found her, I hid the backpack in some bushes. She was in there all day."

That wasn't exactly true. She got out. Who knows, maybe she went home and bothered Dad and came back before recess. It was possible. Maybe after recess, after I tied her in, she squealed so loud that Dad heard her from home. No, that was impossible. Dad has sensitive hearing—*very* sensitive hearing—but no human being could hear a guinea pig from that distance. Nope, she couldn't have bugged him *all* day. So that was my justification for not telling him about the recess parade. Neat, huh?

"So then she wasn't . . . *here*?" Dad said. He sounded like he was talking to himself, so I didn't answer.

His forehead got all worry-lined.

"I'll take her out back and play with her so she won't disturb you anymore," I said.

Dad nodded, then turned away. "Thanks."

I carried my backpack outside and dumped it out onto the grass. Fido ran around in circles, hopping and barking and acting nuts, so I ordered her to sit, and she sat. The people who trained her knew what they were doing. It was a pity we couldn't find the store where Mom bought her. I bet a lot of people in Rustbury would want a trained guinea pig.

Not me, though. I wanted a dog.

Her little turds were hard and didn't smell too bad. Neither did the pee, though it smelled worse. There were some signs of gnawing and scratching on the inside of the bag, but nothing major. I expected it to be worse. Though she shouldn't have stowed away, she had been sort of good. Yes, she did totally embarrass me in front of the entire fifth grade, but that wasn't exactly her fault; I probably left the zipper unzipped. I should try to remember to start closing things I want closed. Such as my mouth around Mom when I want a dog.

Fido sat up, looking up at me, her front paws dangling, her nose and whiskers twitching. All of a sudden, the white mohawk just cracked me up, and I, like, totally lost it. She was a weird, weird little thing, no doubt about it. But she sure did aim to please.

I tossed a twig a couple feet away, and she raced after it. When she brought it back, I threw it again. Then again. And again. Twenty times. Maybe thirty. She was always ready for another toss, hopping up and down, wagging her butt. It wasn't exactly playing Fetch with Buddy. It wasn't *remotely* like playing Fetch with Buddy. But, yeah, okay, in a way, it was Fetch. Fetch with a tiny twig and a rotund rodent.

One time instead of coming back with the twig, she had a dusty old piece of string. She dropped it on the grass then picked up one end in her teeth. The other end dangled.

"You want me to take that?"

She growled. It was a very tiny growl coming from the very tiny throat buried deep in the fur around her neck, but I'm gonna cut her some slack here and call it a growl. I took the other end of the string, and she gripped her end tighter and growled a bit deeper.

"Tug-of-War?" I asked, pulling my end a little harder. "Are you kidding me?"

She dug her front claws into the sod. She wagged her butt, trying to maximize her weight distribution, like a TV wrestler, or least that's what it looked like to me. I tugged a little bit harder. Understand that I was pinching my end of the string between my finger and thumb, and that holding on to it took absolutely no strength at all. This was totally one-sided. She was doing all the tugging.

She dug her claws deeper into the ground and pulled on the string with all her weight. The string snapped between her sharp front teeth, and she rolled over backward like a fuzzy cantaloupe three or four times. It was one of the funniest things I've ever seen in my life. I fell over laughing. I laughed till it hurt. Which felt pretty good. Fido just ran around and around me, squealing.

Dad slid open the window in his study and hollered, "Rufus!"

I stopped laughing. Fido stopped circling. We looked up.

Dad sighed. Then he smiled. I wasn't sure at that distance if it was pleasant or maniacal.

"Never mind," he said, and slid the window shut.

I shrugged at Fido. Did she shrug back? Probably not, but it looked like it.

"Rufus?" a voice called. It came from the front of the house. "Rufus? I don't know the code! Do I need the code?"

It was Lurena Shraits. What was *she* doing at my house?

I ordered Fido back into my backpack and she obeyed without a whimper.

Lurena was on the front porch. She was not hard to spot. Her hair is very long, like, never-been-cut-in-her-life long, and wavy-curly and goldenish. She puts a lot of things in it—girl things, hair things—and she wears really girly clothes, too: dresses, skirts, shiny shoes, sweaters that button down the front. Here's what she doesn't wear: normal clothes, like jeans or athletic shoes or T-shirts or hoodies.

"I really can't knock?" she asked.

"What are you doing here?" I asked.

"I have to have a code?"

"My dad works at home."

"Oh," she said, thinking this over. "I was heading over to the rec center because they started a new Scrabble club, and I came by to ask you to join me, if you'd like. You're the only other person I know who likes to anagram. If you don't go, there might not be anyone there. Except me, that is."

She laughed. Why? Because she thought what she said was funny. She often thinks what she says is funny. And laughs at it. Usually alone.

"So what do you say?" she asked, clapping her hands together. "Want to come?"

It was true that I liked to anagram and that not very many other kids did. But did I want to join a Scrabble club, or hang out with kids who would? More important, was it worth walking down the street with Lurena to check it out? It was the kind of thing that could ruin a fifth-grade guy's image—not that my image was all that hot. Still, I was leaning toward not risking it.

Fido spared me the decision.

14. I guess I forgot to zip it up again.

"So it *is* your guinea pig," Lurena said, looking down at Fido, who had joined us in the front yard. She was standing next to my laceless left shoe, up on her hind legs, looking up at us, her tongue hanging out. She had escaped the backpack yet again.

"You can't bring her to the rec center," Lurena said. "No pets allowed. It's the rules."

"She's not my pet, Lurena," I said. "She . . ." Once again the lie wouldn't come.

"Followed you home?" Lurena said.

"Right."

"What are you calling her?"

"Why do you think she's a girl?"

Lurena set her hand on her hip and rolled

her eyes at me. This was supposed to mean something, I'm sure, but I had no idea what.

"Okay, her name is Fido," I said, "and she's mine, but *please* don't tell anyone, or the guys at school will *kill* me with jokes. Besides, we're not keeping her. My dad hates her. We're taking her back to the pet store . . . as soon as we find it. It was all my mom's idea. I wanted a dog."

Lurena crouched down and put her hand out. The million bangles she always wears on her wrist bangled. Fido sniffed her fingers, then licked them. Lurena giggled.

"Maybe I'll take her," she said. "One of my hamsters died last month."

"What's that mean?"

"It means my chinchilla needs a playmate."

I was getting real nervous standing in my front yard talking to her, *and* doing so with Fido, all in broad daylight. So I asked, "Can we go out back? I don't want anyone to—"

"See you with the G-U-I-N-E-A P-I-G?"

She actually spelled out the whole word. It took an eon.

"Or see you with a G-I-R-L?"

"Just come on."

I set Fido down in the backyard. She warmed up to Lurena pretty fast. It was probably the smell of chinchilla on her.

"How'd your hamster die?" I asked.

"Natural causes."

"Like lightning or something?"

She laughed so hard I about had a heart attack.

"No-wuh! He died of 'old age,'" She made quotes with her fingers. "So you don't want this guinea pig?"

"I told you. I want a dog."

"So then I can have Fido?"

Strangely, I hesitated. I mean, I should have jumped all over that offer. But I said, "I better check with my mom. I think she wants the refund."

Lurena rolled her eyes again. "I will *pay* you for her. Duh."

"Are you rich or something?"

"No, but I have been saving some money

for a replacement since Amherst died."

"Amherst is the hamster?"

"Gee, I don't know. Why don't you anagram it, Mr. Scrabble Expert!"

"Oh. I get it. Good one."

"So do we have a deal? Your mom gets her money. I get Fido. I don't need the cage, though. I have cages. Your mom could get a refund on the cage. What do you say we go talk to your dad about it? He can call your mom. Or does she work at home, too?"

She was so weird. She and Fido belonged together.

"My mom works at Try Your Best Hardware. She'll be home about five thirty or so. I'll talk to her then about it."

Again, the girl rolled her eyes. Maybe they were loose or something.

"All right. Put Fido away then, and let's go to the rec center before it's too late for the Scrabble club."

"I can't leave Fido alone here with Dad. She drives him nuts, remember?"

"Well, you can't bring her to the rec center."

"Then I guess I'll have to take a rain check, Lurena."

She clucked her tongue. "You're goofy, Rufus." She skipped away. "I'll come by in the morning for my guinea pig!" she called over her shoulder.

I was confused for a second how she could be coming by the next morning, then remembered it was Friday, and the next day was Saturday. But I was still pretty confused about a bunch of other things, including why I didn't jump at the chance to unload Fido.

I decided the only thing to do was to get out my bike. Riding it always helped me think. I packed Fido securely into my backpack so I wouldn't come home to a crabby daddy, left a note on the magnetic memo pad on the fridge, went out to the garage, hopped on my bike, and hit the open road.

Maybe it's the freedom to go where you want to as fast as you want to. Maybe it's all the oxygen and the sky and your heart and your muscles all pumping hard. (Yeah, okay, I know your heart *is* a muscle, so that wasn't really necessary to say. But not everybody knows that.) It's so totally amazing that a bike stays up like it does while going so totally fast, and making sharp turns and even catching air, too, if you can do that kind of thing. I can.

It's like when you think about yourself and realize how incredible it is that you can do the things you do all at the same time. Walk, talk, run, eat, taste, see, pedal, jump, kick, blink. The brain is this amazing computer and the body is this incredible machine, and they just run and run and run on, like, fuel that other machines (other people) grow or kill (animals, which are machines, too!) for you. Computers have to be plugged in or have batteries, but we just go and get our own fuel. Our body does, our machine. No machine can move the way ours does. Yeah, there are robots, but no robot can, like, play soccer, even. Or ride a bike as good as me.

Most of the time you don't even think

about how it all works, how your brain and your body are constantly doing all these amazing things. Most of the time you just think about stuff you're not doing, or watch stuff or read or do stuff for school or just hang out. But your computer and your machine are working 24/7.

So what I think happens when you work your body real hard, like riding your bike or playing soccer or whatever, is that you don't have very much energy left over in your brain for other kinds of thinking, like worrying and dreading and stuff. Which is why riding your bike is so good at clearing your head.

Even if all I do is bike around the curvy streets and cul-de-sacs of my neighborhood in the flat little town I live in, my problems start seeming really unimportant and dumb. What if word got out that I had a pet guinea pig? Would I be teased to death? Should I just give—or sell—Fido to Lurena? Why was I even hesitating? Didn't I still want a dog? All these questions buzzed around my brain for the first couple of blocks. Then they didn't, and this is what I figured out:

It was fun being a kid on a bike with nowhere to go. Everything else could wait till my bike and me were back in the garage.

15. I wasn't really thinking about where I was going.

Eventually, I rode by the park. Not that I meant to. Our park had basketball courts and tennis courts and a baseball field and a playground. Tons of kids were there hanging out. I wasn't going to stop. I was happy. But—wouldn't you know it?—my good ole worst friend Dmitri spotted me and started running over. I pedaled faster, but then, realizing he was going to cut me off, I slammed on the brakes, did a one-eighty, and started off in the opposite direction. Big mistake. Before I could get going again, he caught me, grabbed hold of my handlebars, and straddled my front tire.

"Dude!" he said, huffing and puffing in my face. His breath smelled like ranch dressing. "Dude, you seen Murph?"

There are members of tribes living deep in the jungles of uncharted islands in isolated sectors of the South Pacific who have never had contact with the outside world who knew he was going to say that.

"Nope," I replied. "Just out riding. See ya." And I started to step down on my pedal.

That's when Mars galloped up—Mars, the big black puffball of death. His paws were as big as a panther's. His muzzle looked like a lion's. So did his mane. He was as big as a black bear, but only because of the poof. White slobber oozed over his white teeth. And he was unleashed.

"Mars doesn't want you to go yet," Dmitri said.

"No?"

"He wants to know what's in your backpack."

Mars was snarling at my backpack. I felt his hot breath on my neck.

"What's in your backpack, Roof?" Dmitri asked smugly.

"Nothing," I said, though I could feel Fido scrambling around inside it.

"Then why do you have it with you? Why carry an empty backpack around? That doesn't make any sense, dude. And you're supposed to be smart."

"I am? Who says?"

Mars woofed a deep, angry woof, and I felt a hot blast on the back of my arms and neck and head. I almost wet myself. I'm glad I didn't. No one likes that.

Fido barked back, giving herself away, making me a liar. She sounded like a squeak toy, but that wasn't her fault.

"You got that hamster thing in there, don't you?" Dmitri said. He was smiling big now. "The one that chased you at recess. Open the bag, dude. Open it. Mars wants to meet your little friend."

I wasn't about to let Dmitri or Mars meet Fido. I wasn't going to let anyone meet her. It was accidental that she got loose at school, and a mistake that Lurena met her at my house. I needed to prevent anyone else from seeing us together. Especially Dmitri. I would not open my backpack, and that was final. It was my property. Dmitri couldn't just take it and open it without my permission. That was theft and he would have to go to prison, and the law would probably have to put his dangerous dog down. I started to hope he'd try.

And that's when I saw Buddy sprinting across the lawn toward me, black and strong and fast and perfect. Buddy!

"Buddy!" I said. What a dog!

Mars stopped barking and snarling and looked.

Murphy was behind him, waving. "'Sup, dudes!"

Dmitri forgot all about me and Fido and tore off toward Murph.

Mars gave a couple of last sniffs at my bag, then ran after his master. He obviously didn't want to go. He and Buddy did the dog-greeting thing: circling, growling, sniffing, challenging, nipping. Then they relaxed and started play-fighting and racing around with their tongues hanging out and tumbling when they caught each other. I love dogs. If I didn't, I definitely would have done the smart thing and gotten away while I had the chance. Instead, though, I stood there hypnotized long enough for Dmitri to tell Murph about my new pet and to drag him over.

"You keeping secrets from me, Roof?" Murph asked with a grin.

"Nope," I said, glaring at Dmitri.

"Glad to hear it. Wanna play some Frisbee?" He held up a big red one.

I smiled. "Sure!" I sneered at Dmitri.

"What about me?" Dmitri said. "Can I get in on this?"

"Why not?" Murph said. "The more the merrier!"

No one was playing baseball, so we spread out across the grass of the baseball field. I set my backpack down near me. Murphy wound up and threw me an easy, high-flying toss. I caught it, turned, and threw the Frisbee to Dmitri. It sliced a little, and wobbled, and Dmitri had to run a bit to get to it. When he got to it, he bobbled it, then dropped it.

He growled bad words as he picked it up, then turned and hurled it to Murphy. The Frisbee went completely vertical, shot straight up in the air, came straight down, hit the ground ten feet away from Dmitri, rolled a foot, then fell over dead. It was an awful throw. Embarrassing. I knew Dmitri would blame me for it.

"Roof totally threw me off my game, man!" he yelled.

See?

Murph laughed.

"I'm telling you, Murph, he's got that hamster thing in his backpack right now! Check it out! It's, like, his pet!"

"Heads up, Roof!" Murph called, and sent me a perfect flying saucer. It hung in the air over my head a second or two, hovering, then practically lowered itself into my hands, like it had a pilot.

"Sweet!" I said.

"What an insult!" Dmitri said. "That was *totally* awesome, Murph! Maybe the awesomest toss I've ever seen!"

Kiss-up.

"Why, it twarn't nuthin', pards," Murph said, twanging like a cowboy and kicking at a pretend stone.

I threw to Dmitri again, a little more carefully this time. It flew flatter and was right on the money. But he still muffed the catch.

He glanced at Murph, who was waving at a herd of girls walking by.

"Hey, Murph!" he yelled. "Watch the master!"

Murph turned to look. Dmitri wound up, took a couple steps, and unleashed. The disc flew high over my head. It was hooking, so it was moving away from me pretty fast.

Murph laughed and yelled, "Whoa, nice fling, Chuck!"

It was pointless trying to catch it, but I ran after it anyway. I didn't get it.

Fido did.

She came up out of nowhere, scooting fast through the grass, and leaped up in the air and caught it in her tiny rodent teeth. The Frisbee kept flying, spinning her around awhile, before landing softly on the grass. Fido immediately started dragging it across the field to me.

"Whoa, ho, ho, HO!" Murph yelled, running over. "That was *AMAZING!*"

I thought so, too. I mean, the fat little thing *jumped*. She played some serious air! And she *caught* the Frisbee. Like a . . . *dog!* Amazing was exactly what that was.

But wait a minute. . . . Hadn't I sealed her up tight in my backpack before we left home? Maybe I should change her name to Houdini.

The dogs ran over then, Buddy first, because he's faster. I covered my eyes. It would be just my luck that right after discovering my stupid rodent pet had this amazing hidden talent that she would be eaten by my best friend's perfect dog. I peeked through my fingers and watched Buddy circle Fido. Fido marched right up to him and growled her weird buzzy little growl. Buddy growled back and started pawing at the ground. Fido pawed the ground, too. Not as much dirt came up. Then they started sniffing each other, if you know what I mean. To my surprise and relief, Buddy did not eat Fido.

Then Mars arrived.

"Now *this* should be good!" Dmitri said.

Mars joined in on the sniffing and pawing and growling. But, in the end, he did not eat Fido, either. Instead, the three of them ran off together, barking and yapping and nipping at one another, their tongues hanging out of their mouths. They romped. They tumbled. They play-fought. Then Fido chased a squirrel up a tree.

"So what is that thing, Roof?" Murph asked.

"It's my mom's idea of a dog," I sighed.

Murph cracked up. Some best friend.

"It's a guinea pig," Dmitri said with disgust. "Roof has a pet guinea pig! Can you believe that?"

"It's the same one that chased you at school, huh?" Murph asked me.

"I told you," Dmitri answered. "It was in his backpack. It's his little pet. Isn't it, little Doofy–Roofy?"

I ignored him and picked up my backpack. The zipper pulls were still tied together with my shoelace. She hadn't gotten out that way. I turned the bag over. There was a hole the size of a tennis ball gnawed through the bottom.

"Can you believe that, Murph?" Dmitri said again. "I mean, what a total loser. Don't you think, Murph? I mean, a *guinea pig*! Whoa!"

I looked up at Murph. What would he say? Would he make fun of me? He knew how desperately I'd been wanting a dog. Would he laugh at what I got stuck with? Could he be that cruel? Would he go so far as to turn this into one of his big jokes at school? Turn *me* into a big joke?

"I wish I had one," he said.

Good ole Murph.

16. Dinner conversation that night was even weirder than usual.

"A Lurena called for you, Rufus," Dad said. "The number is on the memo board."

I knew what that was about. And I knew what my answer to her offer would be.

"I'll call her back later."

"I think I have a lead on the pet store," Mom said. "Rudy in plumbing said one of the owners was in the hardware store looking for some lighting fixtures because the store was moving to a new, bigger location over in Irondale. He doesn't think it was called Petopia, but couldn't say what it *was* called. I'm still certain it was Petopia. He says the new location is in that little shopping center across from the bowling alley. I think I'll drive over there tomorrow. Who wants to come?"

I didn't. I'd completely changed my mind about returning Fido. But I couldn't get my mouth to say the words. I wasn't ready to give up my dream of a real live dog.

"I don't know if I want to return Fido."

That wasn't me. It was Dad. That's right: Dad.

"Well, knock me down with a feather!" Mom said. "Warming up to her, are you, honey?"

Dad's expression changed from slightly confused and a little embarrassed to mad. "No! She is a ridiculous, noisy nuisance, and a patently absurd idea for a pet."

He noticed Mom looking a little hurt, and added, more gently, "It just doesn't make any sense to me to keep such a thing indoors, or at all . . . in my opinion. That's all."

Mom smiled.

"I don't think I'm following this," I said.

"Well, Rufus," Dad said, looking confused and embarrassed again, "it's just that I don't know if I've been entirely . . . well . . . fair about Fido. Since I started working at home, I've been . . . a bit . . . *tense*, I suppose."

He looked at Mom, and she nodded encouragement. He sighed. Clearly, they'd been having talks.

"I think perhaps I've been too demanding," he continued, "and perhaps too uncompromising, and . . ."

"Crazy?" I suggested.

He glared at me. I was the crazy one.

"You think?" Mom said.

Dad glared at her. Then he sort of grinned.

"Now don't gloat, Raquel. It isn't at all attractive."

Mom straightened her smile into seriousness, and said, "Sorry."

"Well," I mumbled, "I don't want to return her, either."

"Quick! Get the smelling salts!" Mom said, fanning herself with her hand. "I am definitely going to faint!"

"But I still want a dog!" I said over her laughter.

Dad turned to me. His grin disappeared.

"Don't push it, son," he said. "Be happy with what you've got."

"*I'm* certainly happy!" Mom said.

"You're gloating again," Dad said.

"If I keep Fido," I interrupted, "that means I can't ever have a dog, right? Ever?"

"Rufus, if you *don't* keep Fido, you can't ever have a dog," Dad said. "You cannot ever have a dog, Rufus. What part of that sentence do you not understand?"

He can say the cruelest things so casually.

I glanced at Mom. She looked down at her plate. I looked back at Dad.

"Be happy with what you've got," he said again, a little more sympathetically.

"Okay! I'm happy! See!" I pretended to smile, but I'm sure it looked pretty nutty. You know, like when the Joker smiles? "Happy! Happy me! No dog, but I'm happy! I'm happy with what I've got! I've got a guinea pig and no dog! Yippee!"

"You said you wanted to keep her," Mom

said sheepishly. I think I was scaring her a little. Good!

I didn't answer her. I fumed. Fuming feels good—warm and powerful.

"Well, since I won't be going to Irondale tomorrow," Mom said in a come-on-let's-all-cheer-up voice, "how about we go on an outing instead? We could go to the river, to that spot we like. We haven't been there in ages. We could pack a picnic lunch. Maybe go for a hike?"

Dad shook his head. "I didn't get enough work done this week."

"How about Sunday then?"

"Maybe. I'm not promising anything."

"Sunday okay with you, Rufus?"

"Kay-kay," I said. This was the debut of my new "okay."

Dad scowled at me. Shot down again.

"Sunday's fine," I said. "Count me in."

🐾 🐾 🐾

There was a knock on the front door the next morning, which was unusual because of the sign, but not unheard of. Not everybody reads signs, or obeys them if they do.

I poked through the curtains in the living room and saw Lurena standing on the front porch. I had forgotten to call her. Well, I didn't forget. I didn't want to. I was afraid people would find out I called her. I suddenly wished I'd called her, though, because her coming over was way worse. I thought maybe I'd just ignore her, but she knocked again, louder, and I didn't want my dad to get annoyed.

"You didn't call me back," she said when I opened the door. "That was rude."

She was wearing a plaid skirt that touched her shoes, a pink blouse with puffy sleeves, and a vest. She was also wearing a very big hat with lots of fake flowers on it. I scanned the cul-de-sac for anyone who might know me.

"I'm keeping Fido after all," I whispered. *"I have to go inside now. Bye."* I started to close the door.

"Why?" she asked, slapping the door hard with her hand and pushing it open.

"I just . . . *do*," I grunted.

We wrestled with the door.

"Invite your friend in, Rufus," Mom said behind me.

Perfect.

I relaxed my grip on the door and Lurena pushed her way in.

"Thank you, Rufus's mom!" she said, beaming.

"Raquel," Mom said, holding out her hand to shake.

Lurena held out hers, and they shook.

"Lurena Shraits," Lurena said. "I'm in Rufus's class at school."

I peeked my head outside, looking for witnesses to this disaster.

"What is the matter with him?" I heard Mom whisper to her.

"It's okay, Raquel. It's pretty typical behavior for boys his age."

Mom laughed. I didn't. Instead, I put a secret, silent hex on Lurena's tongue and brain.

"Did you know Rufus didn't call me back last night?"

Mom laughed harder.

I wondered if voodoo dolls really worked and how hard it was to make one.

"I told him I would buy Fido from him," Lurena went on. "You see, my hamster, Amherst, died, and my chinchilla, China C. Hill—the C. doesn't stand for anything—needs a playmate, and Rufus said you bought his guinea pig for him because he couldn't have a dog and he didn't really want it and that your husband hates it."

The way Mom kept laughing, she must have thought everything out of Lurena's mouth was hysterical, which was funny, because I sure didn't.

"I didn't say I didn't want her," I said, which was true.

"Maybe not in those exact words," Lurena said, rolling her eyes.

"He's decided to keep her, Lurena," Mom said. "But I'll let you two discuss the matter privately." She looked quickly from Lurena to me with this scary, big smile, like she was hoping we'd get married one day, and I panicked.

"No, Mom! Don't go!"

She pried my fingers off her arm, and said, "Now, you two have a nice chat while I do the breakfast dishes, okay?" Then she left me alone in the living room with a girl.

"The sign's gone," Lurena said.

"Sign?"

"The one on the door. About no knocking. And the code."

"It *is*?"

Dad must have removed it. Only he had that kind of authority. I wondered why he took it down. Was this part of his realizing he'd gone overboard since he started working at home?

"Where's Fido?" Lurena asked.

"Upstairs in my bedr—" I couldn't finish that word. Not to her. "I don't want you to go up—you can't see her right now."

"Can you bring her down?"

"My dad's working." I pointed at his study door, but his BE SILENT OR ELSE! sign, with its headstone with R.I.P. carved into it, was gone, too. "We have to be quiet."

"Oh," Lurena whispered. "Can I see your Scrabble tile collection?"

"It's up in my bedr— I mean, no. Not now. I'm ..." *Think fast, think fast.* "I was just heading over to Murphy's."

"Oh." She looked a little dejected. Then she brightened up. "Can I come with?"

What was the matter with this girl?

"Are you friends with Murph?" I asked her.

"Sure! I've known him since we were babies."

"We're going to ride skateboards. You're not really ... *dressed* for that, are you, Lurena?"

She looked down at her outfit and laughed. "Maybe not! I'll run home and change and meet you over there. Kay-kay?"

That was the nail in the coffin of my new "okay."

"I doubt we'll be at his house long. We'll probably head out right away. You know, riding."

"Where are you going to ride?"

"We never know. Do you even own a skateboard, Lurena?"

"No, but I have inline skates!"

"Nice," I said sarcastically.

"Well, don't worry about me! I'll find you! Even if it takes me all day!"

"Goodie."

She headed for the door. "Bye, Raquel!"

Mom rushed into the room.

Dad opened his door a crack, sighed, then slammed it.

"Sorry, Rufus's dad!" Lurena yelled in a whisper.

"Oh, don't worry about Mr. Grumpy," Mom said, waving her hand in the direction of Dad's study. "Are you going so soon?"

"Just to get my skates. Me and Roof and Murphy are going riding!" She pretended to skate.

"Fun!" Mom squealed.

I closed my eyes and tried to convince myself I was having some terrible nightmare I could not wake myself up from. Then I opened my eyes. No such luck.

Lurena was leaning over, whispering in Mom's ear loud enough for me to hear, *"I get the feeling this was probably the longest playdate Rufus has ever had alone with a girl since he was little."*

Mom laughed.

Playdate?

Lurena and Mom shook hands again.

"It was a pleasure meeting you, Raquel. You have a lovely home."

Kiss-up.

"Thank you, Lurena. And the pleasure was all mine. You are welcome anytime."

Finally, Lurena left, and I resumed normal breathing. Then I punched my mom in the shoulder and ran to my room.

17. I was tired of living in that freak house.

I wanted to live in a normal house. A normal house was a house where . . .

- the dad liked dogs.
- the dad left the house when he went to work instead of staying home all day wearing a suit and fuzzy slippers.
- the dad didn't go on and on about his homemade salad dressings.
- the mom knew the difference between dogs and South American rodents.
- the mom didn't wallpaper the ceilings.
- the dad didn't put a guinea pig in his son's tree house.
- a guinea pig slept in a cage on the

daughter's dresser, not at the foot of the son's bed.

- the son played Fetch, Tug-of-War, and Frisbee with his *dog*.
- strange girls paying uninvited visits were not encouraged by the mom.

But, of course, there was nothing I could do about it. Kids can't pick up, and move. They can't choose where they want to live or who they want to live with. They can't really choose anything. Everything requires permission. We're given choices. Options.

These are your options.

That is not an option.

A dog is not an option. A guinea pig is an option.

You also have the option of a gecko.

I asked my mom if I could go over to Murph's and see what he was up to. She said it was okay with her if it was okay with Dad. Dad said it was okay if I was done with my chores. I wasn't. So I did them. I carried the dirty clothes to the laundry room. I emptied the dishwasher.

I took the garbage out. It was exhausting. Let me make a correction: everything requires permission *and* slave labor.

I put Fido inside my backpack, hopped on my bike, and took off, my muscles aching from all the work. While I was doing my chores, Mom sewed up the hole Fido made in my bag, then reinforced the bottom with a piece of suede. I figured I'd bring Fido along for three reasons:

- Because Dad needed to get some work done before we could go to the river.
- Because Murph liked her.
- Because Buddy did, too.

My idea was that the four of us—Murph, Buddy, me, and Fido—would ride way out past the field around the electrical substation to the woods and go dirt biking. There's a lot of wicked dips and curves and stuff there. I like it better than the skate park, and really nobody goes there but me and Murph.

When I got to his house, I knocked on the door—something, by the way, that Murph's dad has never had a problem with. His mom answered.

"Hi, Rufus!" she said with a nice smile. "It's so good to see you. Come on in. Murph's up in his room."

"Thanks," I said.

That's what I meant when I said normal. It was okay to knock on the door. The mom answers and lets you in without a lot of embarrassing talk. The house was normal, too. It wasn't a mess, but it wasn't superclean like ours always had to be. It looked like people actually lived in it and touched things and stuff. There was a little TV in the kitchen and a big one with a flat screen in the living room, which was usually on even if no one was watching it. Our living room TV was an old box set that we kept in the closet and rolled out on a cart for Family Viewing Time. Honest.

I walked up the stairs and past Murph's little sister's room. A.G. was sitting on the floor reading a book, and I noticed she had socks on her hands.

"Stay back," she said. "I have pox."

"I already had chicken pox," I said.

"So did I. This isn't chicken pox. I believe it's turkey pox, but no one will back me up. The socks are so I won't scratch. Have you had turkey pox?"

"Yes," I lied, and walked on. Annoying little sisters are normal, too, I guess, but A.G. was spoiling my dream house.

Murphy's door was closed. I opened it quietly and peeked in. He was in his room, sitting at his desk, writing. His desk was this really cool tiltable drawing table with a lamp clamped to it. His walls were wallpapered, too, but with pictures he cut out of magazines and newspapers and printed off the Internet— pictures he put up himself, that is. His room was never messy because his mom cleaned it every day. She didn't have a job outside the house. She stayed home and took care of her house and kids. Murph's dad was a foot doctor, so he worked at a doctor's office and at the hospital and made tons of money. He had a workshop in the backyard with power tools and drove a Jeep, not a hybrid, and he had one of those cool Ninja motorcycles. His mom drove a silver minivan. This was Normal House U.S.A.

"'Sup?" I asked.

Murph jumped a little, then shot a quick glance over his shoulder. He flipped whatever it was he was writing, then whipped around, a big, fake grin on his face. Something was wrong.

"Why, 'ello, Rufus, ole chum!" he said with a pretty lame British accent. "Thanks for poppin' by-ee."

"What's wrong?

"Wrong? Why, whatever are you natterin' on about, mate?"

"What's that you were writing?"

Mischief flashed in his eyes—you really had to know him like I did to see it—and he suddenly gave up both the British accent and the chipper act.

"There's no hiding anything from you, is there?" he said glumly. "It's my . . . my . . . well, Roof, it's my last will and testament."

"So you're dying?"

He pretended to be overcome with emotion, then shielded his eyes with his arm. His chin quivered. Oh, he was good.

It was a total crock, of course. Not one of his better crocks, either. I mean, his mom was smiling when she let me in.

"Dude," I said with lots of fake sympathy, "what *izzz* it? What have you got? Or what's got *you*, that is?"

I had high expectations. Murph was no slouch when it came to making stuff up.

"*Anas—*" he said, then broke off coughing. "*Anas tossicus.*"

I shook my head. "What's that?"

"The ducks, man. The *ducks*. At the lake. Surely you remember."

"The poisonous ones?"

He nodded.

"Did you . . . attack one?"

"Accidentally."

"How does that happen, exactly?"

"I rode my board into a flock of them.

They were sleeping on the path. I didn't see them. Whammo! Quack, quack, quack. Envenomization."

"Oh, dear, oh, dear," I said, shaking my head with great fake concern. "I should go down and offer your mom my condolences."

"No," he said, reaching out a hand to stop me. "She . . . she doesn't know yet. I just can't bring myself to tell her. She does love me so . . ."

He set his hand on my shoulder and stared deeply into my eyes, and if I didn't know him the way I did, I probably would have believed he was scared and sick and worried that his poor mom would be grief-stricken. He's that good an actor.

Buddy strolled in then and right away sniffed out Fido in my bag.

"Have you got your guinea pig in there?" Murph said, cheering up. "Take her out!"

I obeyed, and while he and Buddy were fooling around with her, I snatched Murphy's piece of paper. It was not a will, of course. It was just a math handout from school.

"Hey!" Murphy said when he saw what I was doing. "Hand that over!"

He made a grab for it. I held it out of reach.

Buddy barked at me. Fido barked at Buddy.

"Go in the other room, Buddy," Murph said.

Buddy obeyed. Such a good dog! Fido followed after him.

"Be good!" I called after her.

Murph gave me a strange look.

"It's not a will, Murph," I said. "It's homework."

He shrugged.

"What are you doing inside on a Saturday morning doing math, Murph?"

He shrugged again. (Like I said, we shrugged a lot lately.)

"This is *old* math homework, dude," I said. "Like, months-ago homework. Why are you doing it now? And don't you dare shrug again."

"Ms. Charp lost mine so I've got to redo it," he said.

"No way."

"Way."

"She can't do that! It's *her* fault."

"Yeah, tell her that."

I squinted at him. This was more acting.

"Tell me what's going on, dude," I said. "I mean, are we friends or what?"

"Of course we're friends! What a question!"

I give him the Stony Stare. I wasn't putting up with any more of his goofing around.

"Why so serious, Roof?"

Stony Stare.

"Right. Fine. I'm flunking. Happy?"

"Flunking?" The word didn't make any sense coming out of Murphy Molloy's mouth. "Flunking what?"

"What do you think, smart guy?"

I shrugged. "Math?"

"Try again."

I shrugged again.

"Try the fifth grade."

"Yeah, *right*." He's always joking.

"I'm not joking this time."

I squinted at him. If he was acting, he was acting his heart out. No giveaway gestures or sounds. He looked dead serious.

"That's the problem, isn't it, Mr. Boy Who Cried Wolf?" I said. "It's hard to tell when you're serious, because you joke around so much."

"He's not joking." This was his mom. She was standing in the doorway behind me. I guess she was eavesdropping. Parents live to eavesdrop. "He just won't do his work. Nor can he seem to ever get to school on time."

"That's Roof's fault," Murph said, nudging me with his shoulder.

I started to object, but his mom groaned, so I knew I didn't need to.

"I believe it's the other way around," she said.

"I tell you, he's a bad influence, Ma," Murph said. "I was a good kid till he came along, him and his rodent."

"You met Rufus in kindergarten, Smurph. You're lucky to have him. No telling what kind of trouble you'd be in if he didn't keep an eye on you."

Me keep an eye on Murph? Everybody does that. Everybody just watches him. And laughs.

And admires. And gives him free passes.

Not anymore, I guess.

"You got it all wrong, Ma. He always makes me late with his fooling around. And he steals my homework, too. He's a bad kid, Ma. Real bad. A juvenile delinquent." He started to laugh. "With a guinea pig." He lost it.

I didn't think he was being particularly funny.

His mom reached out and pinched his arm.

"Ow!" he howled. "That's child abuse! Roof, you're a witness!"

"You think you can laugh your way out of anything, but I don't think you'll laugh when you end up repeating fifth grade." She wasn't kidding around. "You'd do yourself a big favor to stop joking around and take a page out of Roof's book. He's a good solid student and a true-blue friend. You could learn a lot from him."

What?! Was she nuts? One day in our classroom would have changed her mind about that.

"You're right, Ma," Murph said. "Rufus, will you be my mentor?"

His mom groaned again, then smiled, then giggled despite herself.

"Cute guinea pig, Roof," she said. "I like the hairdo."

And she left the room. Yet another free pass for the Smurph.

"Did you bike here or board?" Murph asked.

"Bike."

"Coolaroni. Let's ride."

"Don't you have to stay here and do homework?"

"Nah. Totally optional."

"You sure?"

"Positootly. Summon the hounds."

Stony Stare. "You know I don't have a—"

"Okay, the hound and the hog."

18. I had no idea guinea pigs could run so fast.

Fido kept up with Buddy. She kept up with my bike! And I didn't take it easy on her, either. I pedaled as fast as I could.

"I'm telling you, Roof!" Murph yelled. "She is the coolest thing on four legs!"

I shrugged, but I was grinning. Ear to ear.

We dumped our bikes in the substation field and played with the dogs. (You know what I mean.) We played Fetch, then Frisbee, then we just let them run around together and hang out and stuff. It was obvious they really liked each other, which was so great. It was what I always dreamed of, minus the guinea-pig part. If Fido had been a golden retriever, it would have been total paradise. I wasn't complaining, though. It was as close to total paradise as I'd ever gotten.

"Let's bike the trails," Murph said.

"Yeah, let's do that!" I said.

Total Paradise 2.0.

We climbed on our bikes and rode for the woods. Buddy and Fido tore after us. Murph slammed on the brakes and skidded in the grass. So I did the same. I wiped out in the grass. Not so cool.

"Stay!" Murph commanded to Buddy, and he stopped in his tracks. What a dog!

"Stay!" I commanded to Fido, and she froze. What a pig!

"Nice," Murph said. "You trained her?"

"Yeah," I lied. I don't know why. Sometimes it's just easy. Sometimes it's just fun. I should probably think about quitting, though. I mean, I know I should tell the truth, blah blah blah . . .

"Sweet," Murph said. "You know, I've been thinking. You wouldn't want to trade, would you?"

"Trade?"

"Yeah."

"Trade what?"

"Fido for Buddy."

I've never fainted before, so I'm not exactly sure how it feels, but I think I almost fainted.

"Shut *up*," I said.

He shrugged.

"You're totally joking." I mean, he had to be.

"You can never tell with me," he said with a smirk.

I squinted at him. Was he joking?

Of course he was!

Wasn't he?

What if he wasn't?

What would I do?

"Think about it," he said. "For now, let's BMX." And he rode off.

I pedaled after him. Buddy and Fido whined a little, but then went back to their playing.

Murph and I rode hard. We screamed into the ditches and caught tons of air when we came back up the other sides, which was fun. Usually we yelled out some monster yell when we lifted off, like *YAARRGGHHRRRR!!!* We both wiped out a bunch of times, which was also fun. We got real sweaty and dirty and scratched up and had, like, the best time of our entire lives.

Then we rode back out onto the field and dumped our bikes and fell on our backs in the grass, laughing our guts out and gasping for breath. Buddy and Fido ran over and mauled us and we rolled around in the grass with them and got all grass-stained and itchy and slobbery, and I understood right then and there what life was for.

When we couldn't take any more pawing and licking, we started throwing things for them to fetch, and the two of them raced after the stuff like they weren't tired in the slightest bit. Dogs are great. They're gods—anagrammed, anyway. I wondered what guinea pigs anagrammed was. I started working on it in my head, but that made me think of Lurena: Lurena looking for us; Lurena finding us; Lurena ruining paradise.

I hated Lurena.

"Why do you like girls?" I asked Murph.

He laughed. "You don't?"

"No. If there was a girl here, she'd wreck everything. Girls don't understand stuff like this."

"Some of 'em do. There's all kinds of girls, Roof. And all kinds of guys."

"That's true. Like Dmitri."

He laughed again. "Yeah. Do you like Dmitri?"

"*Like* is such a strong word."

Again he laughed. Laugh, laugh, laugh. What a happy guy.

"I don't think it matters that much if a kid is a guy or a girl," he said.

"It just matters what's *inside*?" I said in a deep, teacherlike voice. He couldn't be serious with that cornball stuff.

"Look at Fido," he said, pointing.

I looked. She was fighting over a stick with Buddy and growling like a bulldog.

"You can't judge a book by its cover, et cetera, et cetera," Murph said.

Exactly, I thought. Here he was, my idol, the guy with the perfect dog, the normal house, and the great parents, and he was flunking, and he wanted to trade his perfect dog for a guinea pig with a mohawk. Was no one what they seemed?

Maybe Dmitri was different, too, "inside." And Lurena. I was different than what the kids at school thought I was. I wasn't sure what they thought I was, but chances were they didn't really know who I was, mostly because I hid who I was so they wouldn't laugh at me. Maybe other kids did that, too.

Was that why Murph had so many friends? Did he somehow understand better than other people that nobody was what they showed on the outside, that everybody had good stuff on the inside, but a lot of it got all twisted up on the way out because people also were trying to be cool and popular?

It's not as if Murph didn't care about being cool or popular. He sure liked attention. He liked it so much, he didn't care who paid it to him. It made him happy. And people like happy people.

Now he was in trouble, bad trouble, which

had to make him sad, and he was hiding it. Why? Maybe he was afraid people wouldn't like him as much if he wasn't happy.

I didn't want to spoil our fun by bringing all this up, but, as his friend, I thought I should.

"You're going to have to work hard to catch up in school."

He nodded. "You're going to help me, right?"

He seemed serious, which was suspicious.

I nodded. "Sure, yeah. Of course."

He grinned. "Cool. I don't want to repeat. That would mean we wouldn't be in the same grade next year. Which would make me cry."

I smiled. "Yeah, it totally would."

"Totally," he said with a laugh, then he punched me in the shoulder.

I punched him back, then Buddy and Fido saw us punching each other and ran over and piled on top of us.

Total Paradise 3.0.

19. If I made the laws, Mom would have been arrested.

Why? She invited Lurena to come to the river with us on Sunday. She did it behind my back and without my permission.

"I'd rather invite Murphy," I told her.

"Go ahead!" she said. "The more the merrier!"

I shuddered at the thought of the three of us crammed into the tiny backseat of one of our hybrids. No doubt I'd be in the middle, pressed up against Lurena.

"Never mind," I said.

"Lurena said to be sure to bring Emmeline along," Mom said with a smile.

"*Fido*, Mom!" I yelled. "It's *Fido! Fido, Fido, Fido!*"

She jumped half a foot in the air.

"I think the animal's name is Fido, Raquel," Dad said. "And isn't this supposed to be a pleasure trip, a time for rest and relaxation? How am I supposed to relax with a squealing pig around?"

I thought this might be my out.

"I'll stay home with Fido so you can relax, Dad."

"No," Mom said. "If Dad refuses to let her come with us, then I suppose we will have to leave her behind."

She looked at Dad with her head tilted slightly. Mom's head tilts were worth a thousand words. In this case, they meant, *If you do not object to what I just said, I won't speak to you for hours, if not days.*

"Fine," Dad said. "Bring her. But keep her quiet, Roof."

"It's Mom who wants to bring her," I said. "And it's not fair, Mom. Dad deserves some downtime from work to commune with nature. I really think I should stay home with Fido so she doesn't drive him nuts. You'll just have to call Lurena and tell her Fido and I won't be going."

Mom smiled at me. Would it kill her not to see through me every once in a while?

"This is a family picnic," I moaned. "Lurena is not part of our family."

Mom laughed. I once heard a comedian on a talk show say that other people's pain is funny. Mom must agree.

"Lurena is your guest," she said.

"*You* invited her, not me."

"Tone, Rufus," Dad said. "Keep it respectful."

"She didn't even ask me, Dad!"

"Really?" Dad said, looking at Mom. "In that case, I believe she is your guest, Raquel, this little Miss What's-Her-Name."

"Lurena," Mom said. "And I was just being hospitable. She's so polite and so eager to be friends with Rufus."

"Oh, yeah?" I said. "Well, maybe I'm not so eager to be friends with *her*. Ever think of that?"

"*Tone*, Rufus," Dad said again.

Mom sank into a chair and rubbed her forehead with her fingers.

I flashed back to my talk with Murph out on the substation field about books and their covers.

"Okay, fine," I said. "But next time, ask, okay?"

Mom cheered up. Murph needed a mom like mine. No free passes with her.

🐾 🐾 🐾

"It's very conscientious of you to own a hybrid, Raquel and Art," Lurena said.

"Thanks, Lurena," Mom answered. "Actually, we own two. Do your parents have one?"

"Yes, they do. They also have an electric car for local trips."

Lurena was sitting behind my mom, who was driving. I was behind Dad. Mom always drove. Dad liked having the time to think. Plus, since she actually went places, Mom was the more practiced driver.

Fido was standing in my lap, her front paws

pressed against my door, her tongue and wagging, craning to try to see out the window. Her claws were making little squeaking noises on the upholstery.

"Rufus, can you make Fido stop making that noise?" Dad said. "It's like nails on a chalkboard to me."

"You're close, Art!" Lurena said, laughing. "Nails on a car door! Ha!"

Mom laughed. Only Mom. Well, Mom and Lurena.

"Down," I said to Fido. She looked at me with an expression like, *Really? Do I have to?*

"Down," I said again.

She pouted and climbed down into my lap. I scratched her behind the ears to cheer her up. It worked. She fell asleep.

"Did you train her yourself?" Lurena asked. I didn't, but I nodded.

"What other commands does she know?"

"*Kill,*" I whispered.

"Do you think you're funny?" she asked with a squint.

"*Fido, kill!*"

ke up and snarled at her. This
rena. It might even have scared her
nd. I enjoyed that.

ay, Fido. Down, girl. Down. Good girl."

ratched her neck.

"You're kind of a psycho," Lurena said.

"Takes one to know one," I said.

🐾 🐾 🐾

Mom chose a picnic table and started setting up lunch. Lurena offered to help and pretty soon was talking Mom's ear off. Dad set up a lounge chair and stretched out on it and started reading some book—his idea of outdoor fun. Fido and I slipped away without anyone seeing us. In this case, the *less* the merrier.

So I wasn't Murphy, or Mom. Did I ever say I was? Do we all have to be?

Fido and I walked down the steep path toward the river. You could really tell spring was coming, because everything was turning green and smelled damp. It was great. I felt totally alone in the wilderness, just me and my . . .

It was no use. I tried to put the word *dog* in there, but I just couldn't.

There was no getting around it. Fido was a rat. A big, fat orange rat with a spiky white mohawk and creepy toes. No matter what Murphy said about her, no matter if he would really trade Buddy for her (no way), no matter how much Buddy or Mars liked her, she wasn't a dog. She never would be. Yeah, she acted like one. A lot like one. Incredibly like one. But she wasn't one. She was a guinea pig. I could pretend I was this supercool, superdeep, totally open-minded dude who would be just as happy with any pet so long as it played games, learned tricks, ran alongside your bike, and loved you more than anyone in the whole world. You know, a dude like Murph. I could pretend I'd be happy with an iguana that played Tug-of-War, or a parrot that slept at the foot of my bed, or a goldfish that caught Frisbees. But that wasn't me. Bottom line: I wanted a dog.

But I couldn't have one. So I was making lemonade out of my fuzzy, fat lemon. If Dad could learn to live with her, if Murph could wish he had one just like her, if Buddy the perfect dog could make her a buddy, I guess I could learn to put my dreams away forever and try to accept her for what she was: a guinea pig that acted a lot like a dog. That was better than a dog that acted a lot like a guinea pig, wasn't it? Yeah, sure, she definitely was. She was better than *that* kind of dog, anyway.

Fido ran after some ducks on the bank of the river, and, for a second, I worried they might be poisonous. She barked at them, though, and they flew off, quacking. She enjoyed this so much, she went off hunting for more.

Later, we played Crocs-in-the-Nile, which was a game I'd been playing since I was a little kid. The river was pretty shallow where we were and had big rocks in it poking out of the water. The object of Crocs-in-the-Nile was to jump from rock to rock without falling. If you fell into the water, that meant you were croc chow. For the first time in a long time, I had someone new to play the game with. I usually played with Mom.

Fido followed after me at first, jumping the same rocks as me, and she was really good. She scrambled a lot when she landed on the rocks, which were slimy and slippery with green goo, but she never fell in the water. After a while, she was hopping around like nobody's business and leading the way. In fact, she won the game.

Why? Because I fell in and twisted my ankle. Hard. I couldn't even stand up on it. So I sat down on a rock with my feet in the water. The coldness felt good on my ankle, though the pain was still intense. The pain was shooting up my leg, probably toward my heart. I figured I didn't have long to live.

I looked at the wilderness around me. Fido was hopping up and down on the shore, barking and whining hysterically.

I had only one hope.

"Go get help, Fido!" I commanded. "Get help! Go on! Get help, girl! Get help!"

In hindsight, I was probably slipping into shock.

Fido stopped barking and concentrated on

my words or my tone or my face or something. She was very concentrated. Then she chirped, nodded quickly, and tore off in what looked like the right direction. I hoped help would arrive soon or I'd be a goner.

A couple of minutes went by before it dawned on me that I was waiting to be rescued by a guinea pig. I began dragging myself toward the shore. This was not turning out to be the funnest picnic of my life.

Before I got far, Fido returned—*YAY!* She was barking like crazy, and being followed by Lurena. My heart sank. Why did I have to be saved by *her*?

Lurena was smirking, and I imagined the horror of this scene being told and retold at school.

But Mom showed up a minute later, and I felt better. For about a second.

"Oh, Rufus!" she bawled. "Thank God! Oh, my poor, poor baby!"

Lurena's smirk widened.

Fido got to me first. She bounded up, bursting

with pride, then leaped from the bank and landed on my chest, digging her claws into my shirt—and, through it, into my flesh—to hold on. Big ouch. I didn't complain, though. I was too darn proud of her. She scrambled up my chest (which hurt more) and licked my face.

"That's my good girl!" I said, laughing. "Good girl!"

20. I didn't break my ankle.

I broke my foot. Murph's dad fixed it. He's a foot doctor, remember? That meant a cast, of course, and crutches. I had to stay home from school for a week—Mom's orders, not the doctor's. She wanted me to stay in bed as much as possible and keep the foot "elevated." The crutches were to get me to the bathroom.

Fido kept me company, and she was a real pal. She played games with me and did tricks and fetched things for me, like comic books and the remote. (Mom brought the TV and DVD player in from the family room to help keep me in bed.) I trained Fido to take out discs and put in new ones. It was pretty cool. She curled up in bed with me, too, watching the movies. She seemed to like comedies the best, especially if they had dogs in them. She hissed at any cats that showed up.

Lurena came over sometimes, and when I was bored, I actually let her come up to my room and we played Scrabble. Why not? I figured. She'd already wrecked my life at school anyway by telling everyone about her going on a picnic with me, about me owning a guinea pig, and about Fido saving my life. She was pretty impressed with the tile collection, but felt it should be cleaned and organized, so I let her do that. I figured she owed me. She also liked my collection of paint stirrers with anagrammed Scrabble tiles glued onto them, and made a few of her own. Her anagrams were very different from mine. Mine were like: SLOW KELP KILL CRAB LIPS and POISON FART BISON; hers were like: LIMP SHRILL HUM IS NIGH and AN OWL ROMP A JAM LOVER.

Sometimes she brought China C. Hill, her chinchilla, along to keep Fido company. China C. was about the same size as Fido, but more mouselike, with big ears and a tail. She had a weird, wrinkly gray coat and often stood up on her hind legs. She was always really nervous.

Fido was pretty mean to her. Usually she growled and barked at her and chased her under my bookshelf, where China C. remained the rest of the visit. Lurena said it was just a game they played, but I was pretty sure Fido was trying to catch China C. and eat her, even if Fido wasn't much bigger.

One time, Lurena said, "I'm still willing to buy Fido from you. China C. really likes her. And I think the feeling is mutual."

At the moment, China C. was cowering under the bookshelf, and Fido was on the floor nearby, waiting.

"I'm not willing," I said.

"I'll double what I was going to pay you before."

"No deal."

"Triple?"

"Nope."

"I'll throw in China C."

"Fido's not for sale. She's mine. End of discussion."

Lurena grinned at me.

"Glad to hear it," she said, like that was what she wanted to hear all along.

Girls.

🐾 🐾 🐾

One day, Mom said Dmitri was at the door.

"Don't let him in," I said.

"Ohhh," she said. "Sorry . . ."

Dmitri stepped by her through the door and started scanning the room like he was going to be making a full report at school the next day.

"Hey, Roof," he said. "How's the . . . ?"

He looked stuck. I helped him out.

"Foot?"

"Yeah."

"Still broken."

He continued his scanning, like he wasn't finding what he was looking for. Then I caught on.

"You looking for Murph?"

"Yeah. He here?"

"He was, but he left."

"Where to?"

"Park, I think."

"I bet you wish you could go to the park, huh?" He grinned.

What a nice guy. "I bet you'd win that bet."

"I guess I'll head over there," he said. "I got something to show him."

"What is it?"

"I said I got something to show *him*."

I repeat: what a nice guy.

"But, look, uh, I got this for you." He dug into his pocket and pulled out something. It was a small gray gadget with a little screen. "It's my old Game Boy. I don't use it anymore, and my mom thought I should give it to you since you're stuck at home and all."

"Your mom thought?"

"Yeah. I guess she knows your mom and they were talking, yap yap yap. You know."

I nodded. I knew.

"I'm doing PSP now, so I don't need it. Some of the buttons kind of stick, but it works okay."

"Gee, thanks, Dmitri," I said, trying not to sound too sarcastic.

"Like I said, my mom thought it might help you pass the time, you know, while you're sick."

"It's not that bad, really. I have movies and books and . . ." I glanced at Fido sleeping at the foot of my bed. She was snoring and pawing at the air. Probably dreaming she was running.

"And your *guinea pig*." He said it like he was talking about a turnip-asparagus-booger smoothie.

"Yeah, my guinea pig, Fido." I tapped my thigh. "Here, Fido! Here, girl!"

"Fido," Dmitri snorted. "You're a total dork-chop, dude."

Fido woke up, panted, then scampered up to my chest and sat, waiting for my next command.

"What the—?" Dmitri said, then a laugh burst through his lips.

"Roll over," I said to Fido.

She rolled over, then popped back up to her feet. I peeked at Dmitri out of the corner of my eye. His smugness faded a little.

"Good girl," I said, and scratched her head. "Play dead."

She dropped onto her back and went limp. Her tongue fell out her mouth.

Dmitri let slip a little "Whoa."

"Good girl, Fido," I said, and she jumped back to her feet. I fed her one of the bacon bits I kept under my pillow. "Remote, Fido."

She fetched it. I pushed the EJECT button and the disc in the player across the room ejected.

"Disc out," I said.

She dove from the bed, dashed across the carpet, ducked under the disc, poked her nose up into the hole, then carried it to me. I put it in its case, popped out the disc from another one, and held it out to her.

"Disc in."

She scooped it with her snout, took it to the player, and deposited it into the slot.

"Oh, man!" Dmitri said. "I *so* want one of those!"

This was satisfying, but irritating as well.

"She's one of a kind, dude," I said.

"No such thing."

I thought of a pretty cornball thing to say about how everybody's one of a kind, but figured he'd just make fun of it, so instead I held up the movie case and said, "Have you seen this? It's pretty funny."

"Yeah," he said, "but I'd watch it again."

I pressed PLAY on the remote and the FBI warning came on, then a bunch of previews.

"Hit MENU, dude," Dmitri said.

"I like watching previews."

"Dorkchop," he muttered.

After the previews, the movie started. Fido curled up in my lap, and Dmitri sat on the floor at the end of my bed. About halfway through, Dmitri called real quietly, *"Here, Fido!"* She looked up at me for an okay, and I nodded, so she went to him. I figured I should share. I heard Dmitri giving her commands and laughing and playing with her.

I'd seen the movie, so I fooled around with the Game Boy. It was old school, and the buttons actually stuck pretty bad, and it was his mom's idea to give it to me, but he was acting nice and friendly, and he had even changed his mind about Fido. That was a start. Look how long it had taken me.

"What's this? Dmitri playing with a rodent at Roof's house while his dog is tied up outside and howling to wake the dead?"

Dmitri and I turned and saw Murph standing at the door. He was smiling, of course. Dmitri jumped up like the floor was on fire and dropped Fido like she was suddenly electrified.

"H-Hey, Murph, dude!" he said. "'Sup? What're *you* doin' here? Want to go hit the skate park, man? Catch some air?"

Murph nodded. "Sounds sweet. Definitely sweet. But don't let me interrupt this touching scene. What're you guys watching?"

I held up the movie case.

"Cool," Murph said. "Count me in. But, Dmitri, you've got to do something with Mars. He's miserable."

"You got Buddy with you?" Dmitri asked.

"No, I leave Buddy at home when I come to Roof's." He looked at me and smiled. "The dude's dad doesn't like dogs."

"Really?" Dmitri said, acting like he had wandered into Freak Land. "I did not know this. I'll call home and have someone pick up Mars." He pulled out his U-phone and started punching buttons. "I didn't think I'd be staying. I was hoping to find you and we'd hit the park or something, dude. I'm still up for it. I'm ready to go. . . ."

"After the movie," Murph said.

"You know, Murph," I said, "I've seen it before, and so has Dmitri, and to tell you the truth, I could use some sleep."

"You sure, man?"

"Positootly."

"You da boss, Roof. Broken-foot guy. *Vamos*, Señor Sull."

"Huh?" Dmitri said, one ear still on the phone.

"I have your homework," Murph said to me, and held it up. "For after your siesta. With Ms.

Charp's compliments. She says she misses you and she loves you and get well soon."

I squinted at him. Did she really say that?

"Shireen and Keisha said the same thing," he said.

Okay. Nobody said any of that.

Murph slapped Dmitri's shoulder with the back of his hand. "Go shut up your dog, dude. I'll be right down."

"Righteous," Dmitri said. He dumped his phone in his pocket and hustled out the door.

"He didn't even say good-bye," I said, faking a pout.

"To you or to Fido," Murph added, and covered his heart with his hand. "Has the boy no feelings?"

"No, he doesn't. He gave me his old busted Game Boy. His mom made him." I held it up for him to see.

"He's learning the meaning of sacrifice. That's important. He's growing."

I laughed.

"So what's up with him and Fido anyway?"

"Weird, huh? He wants one, too."

"You are a trailblazer, Roof. A trendsetter. Guinea pig sales will go through the roof."

"You gonna come back and do homework with me?" I asked.

"I guess I better."

"You better."

"Okay, okay. Cease cracking the whip, taskmaster."

"Were you on time for school today, young man?"

"Yes, Mother dear. Teacher gave me a gold star."

"Prove it."

"She put it in her grade book."

"Prove it."

He rolled his eyes.

"You were late," I said.

"I was not."

"How late?"

"A couple of minutes. So what?"

"So what? That's three times this week, and it's only Wednesday."

"Yeah, but let me tell you what happened on the way to school. . . ."

"Save it, Murph."

He acted all hurt.

"Till later," I said. "Dmitri's waiting. You can tell me when you come back—*after* we finish our homework."

"Yes, Sarge. See you at sixteen hundred hours, more or less."

"Isn't that four o'clock? Because it's already past that...."

"Never mind. Over and out." And he left.

I looked around for Fido. She was actually right under my nose, on my chest. She must have curled up there when I was talking to Murph. I scratched her head. People came and went, but she was always there.

"What do you say?" I said. "*Lassie* again?"

It was her favorite, even if it wasn't exactly mine.

She panted.

"Okay," I said, pressing EJECT on the remote. "Disc out."

21. Every kid dreams of getting crutches.

But as a kid who has had them, let me tell you: you don't want them.

The first day I was released from bondage was a Saturday, and I couldn't wait to take Fido for a walk. Mom had bought a ferret collar and leash from a different pet store she found. She never did find Petopia, or whatever the store she bought Fido from was called. Because of this, and the doggish way Fido turned out to be, she tried to convince Dad and me that the place was some kind of enchanted, magical place where wishes were granted. Dad didn't believe her one little bit. Me? I believed her a little bit more than he did.

Mom also bought a tiny cat tag and had Fido's name and our address and phone number inscribed on it. And she bought a couple of rawhide bones, some squeeze toys, and a ball launcher and a couple of little pink rubber balls to launch. I thought she'd gone over the top, but Fido was so happy she peed herself.

I attached the tag to the collar and put the collar around Fido's neck. I kept quiet around Fido about what sort of animal the tag was made for. She kept tugging at me on the walk, even though I was walking on crutches outside for the first time. She insisted on sniffing everything on both sides of the sidewalk, especially the stuff just out of her reach.

"Will you give me a break?" I pleaded. "I'm on crutches here."

She didn't care.

I only fell four times.

When we got home, I took her out back and unhooked her. She ran around in circles like a mad dog. I hobbled into the garage to my dad's workbench and opened his toolbox. Both the bench and the box were covered with dust and cobwebs. I found some boards and a saw and a sawhorse and carried them over to my work area, which wasn't easy with the crutches, but somehow I got them there. Fido came in and crawled up on the bench and watched me, which made it more fun. I measured and sawed and hammered, and then I heard a voice behind me.

"What are you up to, son?"

"Sorry, Dad. Am I being too noisy?"

He shook his head. "Need any help?"

I shrugged. "Sure."

He was actually a big help. It wasn't too long before the doghouse was built. We painted it white with a red roof, then we went out in the yard while it was drying.

Dad dug some golf tees out of his pocket and tossed one. Fido raced after it.

"I think it's going to work out after all," Dad said.

"What is?" I said.

"Working at home."

"Oh. How come?"

He shrugged. "I just needed some time to adjust. To change my way of thinking. To look at it differently."

He looked at me and smiled.

"These help," he said, and pulled some orange earplugs out of his pocket.

I smiled. "I bet. Good idea."

Fido retrieved the tee, and Dad threw another one.

"You happy with your pet?" he asked.

"Yep," I said.

"I'm glad. I like her, too. She keeps me company. It gets lonely in this big house all day by myself."

I nodded. I hadn't thought about that.

"I'm not going to walk her, though."

"I know."

"Or clean up her . . . messes."

"Check."

"And you need to keep her away from my shoes."

"You should keep your shoes away from her," I said.

"You're probably right about that."

Fido came back again, and Dad scooped her up. It was wild to watch him with her. He was petting her and cooing and rubbing his nose in her fur. Weird.

But then he stopped all of a sudden and took off his glasses. He leaned in real close and squinted, then picked something out of her fur with his finger and thumb. His face scrunched up, and his eyes burned with fury. He shoved whatever he had pinched in his fingers in my face and bellowed, "FLEA!"

🐾 🐾 🐾

Mom was sent back to the new pet store to buy flea killer. Meanwhile, Dad stomped around the house, vacuuming all the carpets and furniture and washing all the rugs and bedding. I was ordered to give Fido her first bath, outside.

When Mom returned, she came out to help.

"We can only give her just a teeny bit of this stuff," she said. "It's made for C-A-T-S, which weigh more."

I nodded. And I appreciated her spelling out the C-word. Fido was freaked out enough as it was.

"Dad's pretty mad, huh?" I asked.

"Oh, I don't know. I think he likes housework. He sees the fleas as invaders, and he's protecting his home. Big hero!" She laughed.

"Really? I don't think he likes housework."

"You're probably right," she said.

We bathed Fido in a soup pot in the backyard. She looked even more ratlike when wet. But even dogs look weird when they're soaked to the skin. What was more upsetting was how miserable she looked. She was shivering like crazy. And she sure was giving me the stink eye.

"Time to get her out of there," Mom said, and lifted her out onto the towel we had ready.

I bundled her up and held her to my chest to warm her. She was trembling like a leaf. Her teeth were chattering.

Mom's bottom lip stuck out, her chin quivered, and her eyes got all moist. I knew what that meant.

"Don't, Mom," I said.

"I can't help it," she said, and sniffled. "It's just so *sweet*."

"Stop, Mom."

"The two of you . . . ," she went on.

"Mom, I mean it!"

"Okay, okay, sorry." She wiped her wet nose with her sleeve.

I shook my head. How hopeless was this woman? She brought me home a guinea pig instead of a dog. She said it would be quiet and it wouldn't chew things up and it would bathe itself. She said that it wouldn't get fleas. *Hah!* She was so wrong. Wrong, wrong, wrong, wrong. About everything!

Well, not about one thing, I guess. She said she knew I'd love Fido.

So I tossed her a bone.

"Thanks, Mom," I said. "You know . . . for Fido."

"Oh, you're welcome, sunshine!" she said. Then she busted out bawling.

I tell you, when it comes to moms, sometimes it's best just to keep your thanks to yourself.

After Fido was dry and happy, I went into the garage and finished the last detail on her doghouse. No doghouse is complete without the name painted in an arc over the door, right? So I did that, then I carried the house outside under my arm.

Fido got so excited she jumped up and down till she knocked it out of my hands. I tried to catch it and got tangled up in my crutches and fell on the ground. It was lying on its side, so I tipped it upright. Fido ran in and out and in and out and in and out, like she knew exactly what it was and who it was for. Then she walked around it a few times and marked it, if you know what I mean. When she was done with that, she went inside, turned around, and plopped down. All that was outside was her head resting on her paws. She looked so happy. Which made me happy. Crippled and sprawled out on the grass with my crutches, but happy.

I remembered then that I put a treat in my pocket for her for after the bath, and I dug it out. It was a rawhide bone from the new pet shop. When Fido saw it, she sprang from her house, poised for action, her nose high, her butt wagging. I tossed the bone up over her head. She leaped, caught it in midair, and came down with it. Then she ran over to me.

"Good girl!" I said, scratching her neck. "Attagirl! Whattagirl! That's my girl!"

She soaked up the praise awhile, then darted off to some bushes, where she dug a hole, dropped in the bone, and buried it.

What a dog!

Patrick Jennings is the author of many books, including the critically acclaimed *Faith and the Electric Dogs*, *The Beastly Arms*, and *We Can't All Be Rattlesnakes*. He lives with his family in Washington State. You can visit his Web site at www.patrickjennings.com.